EIVOR

and

THE BLADES OF HADES

HARSIMRAN SIDHU

BlueRose ONE.com
Stories Matter
NewDelhi • London

BLUEROSE PUBLISHERS
India | U.K.

For permissions requests or inquiries regarding this publication, please contact:

BLUEROSE PUBLISHERS
www.BlueRoseONE.com
info@bluerosepublishers.com
+91 8882 898 898
+4407342408967

ISBN: 978-93-5989-458-4

Cover design: Shivam
Typesetting: Namrata Saini

First Edition: July 2024

RECAP

Aetios, Percy, Eivor, Atreus, and Nathan were teenagers from Sparta, but one day their lives changed. They found out about a prophecy, Deimos, the evil one was free once again and this time it was up to them to find and collect god's weapons to fight him. Firstly, Aetios had to find the Spear of Leonidas. The team embarked on an adventurous quest to find it but when they met Deimos they realized they were severely underpowered. Fortunately, with the help of the spear, they made it out alive but now they have to find all the other weapons before the blood Moon if they want to win against Diemos.

CONTENTS

Chapter 1

THE FORGER OF LAMIA

Those rousing words by Aetios had left everyone unmovable. It was like they were frozen, like they had experienced a whole ice age. Percy said in a slightly breathy voice, “So, where to now?” Aetios turned and looked directly into his eyes and said, “I need to meet an old friend, in Lamia.” Nathan was furious, as he knew if they were to travel to Lamia they would be in the heart of the Peloponnesian war. He said in an unsteady voice, “I think we should not go there unless you have a death wish.” Aetios’s decision was firm, he knew that if anyone in the world could help them, then, it would be none other than Vulcan. Aetios slowly walked towards his horse and said, “There is no other way, Nathan.” Everybody got on their horses and they were off to Lamia, north-west of Thermopylae, it was a mammoth city.

The young heroes galloped through the wild woods and reached Lamia within a night. As they got out of the woods, the view was magnificent. A bridge stood enveloping the river from the top and across it were the huge gates of the marvelous city. It was unbelievable, such a beautiful city amid a cruel war. The fortified capital was a work of art, one could do nothing but admire the beauty of it, so did Atreus and Eivor when Percy came from behind and said, "Don't just admire it from the outside, let's go in." They reached those enormous gates which looked even bigger from near. The guards were wearing black and red armor with a sheathed sword and a spear in their hands, maybe some hidden knives too, who knows? They stopped Aetios who was walking in front of everyone and asked, "What is your business here, boy?" Eivor shouted from behind the group, "We just want to meet Vulcan, that's all." The guards were a bit confused and said in a sarcastic voice, "What in the world would you want from that drunkard." Aetios unanticipatedly pulled out his spear, put it to the throat of that guard, and said in a harsh voice, "Don't you dare disrespect him." The other guard was about to strike him with his spear when Percy pointed Hofund towards him and warned him, "I would not try that if I was you." The guard looked nervous, he withdrew his sword. Aetios could not bear any words said against Vulcan. The guards finally let them in, as they entered the city, huge buildings and temples could be seen from a distance, and numerous vendors were roaming around the streets. It was a very happy sight. Stone roads, high walls, and an atmosphere they had never seen before. People were roaming with their families and looked very friendly. Percy said, "So, where was his house." "We'll ask someone here", replied Aetios. Everyone seemed to know him quite well. We went up to a fruit vendor and Percy asked as he picked up an apple from his shop, "Hey you, do you know where Vulcan lives?" He replied, "Vulcan, the blacksmith? He lives in the far east of the city in a lonely place. The only person mad enough to live there is him, in between those creepy fields." Aetios and Percy looked at each other with suspicion and said simultaneously, "A blacksmith? Are you sure we are talking about the same guy, he is middle-aged with long grey hair, half of his teeth missing and slightly bent foraward." "Yes I could never forget that freak", replied the vendor. Aetios again was a bit angry but he held his anger as he closed his fist tightly and gave him a deadly stare. "We can reach there before noon if we are quick" added Nathan. They got on their horses again and rode east towards his dwelling, Aetios could not wait to meet his old friend, he was looking up into the sky while riding.

They got there in a few hours as they were not allowed to ride fast inside the city. It looked like an abandoned house from a distance, it had a cone-shaped roof with red and white color on its walls. It was the only structure in about three to four acres of plain land. Upon reaching its door they saw a wolf symbol on it, but it was different from one they had seen before. It had a scar in its left eye, it looked menacing. Percy knocked on the door and said, "Vulcan, open the door." A crooked and barely audible voice spoke, "Don't you brats dare knock on my door." "You remember my name, don't you?" replied Aetios. He again spoke in a rather uncomfortable voice, "How would I know if you wouldn't tell me?" Aetios again said in a calm voice, "Aetios." There was an unusual silence for a moment and then Vulcan spoke again, "Go away, what do you want now after so many years of absence? I will not listen to a single word from you and if that angry sod is also with you, tell him to jump off a cliff and die." Percy was furious and tried to barge into the door but Eivor had to stop him. Aetios again said very calmly, "We need your help, we need to save Greece." "Save Greece, again? I don't have such free time", replied Vulcan. Eivor was hopeless of getting any kind of help from him, he walked back and sat on the fields where the wind blew heavily and the grass was very tiny as if someone had cut it very carefully. Eivor was lying there looking up into the cloudy sky when Atreus came running towards him and said, "I can hear horses galloping towards us, thousands of them. Nobody believes me." Eivor knew Atreus had a distinctive hearing ability, he quickly got up and tried to look across the fields but could not see anything. He rushed towards Aetios, grabbed his shoulder, and said, "We need to go, the Athenians are coming." Aetios did not believe as he thought Eivor was too gullible. Suddenly Ikaros came down screeching and sat on Aetios's shoulder, they knew something was coming their way. His mood changed drastically and was now looking very serious. Percy was listening to all of this very carefully, he said in a proud voice, "If they are here to fight, I think we should give them what they want." Aetios had a different opinion, if they were coming to take over Lamia, the king might be interested in helping. Aetios said suggestively, "We need to get to the palace quickly and inform the king about it." Percy agreed but he was not about to request someone, he said coldly, "I will meet you at the entrance of the city. You should go and ask the king for help." Aetios agreed as it was pointless arguing with someone like Percy. They rushed to the king's palace, it again took them quite a time to reach there. The entrance had a huge hidden gate with two guards standing in front of it. Eivor said, "We need to meet the king, right now." The guard replied in an angry voice, "The king doesn't meet kids like you." Eivor was furious, he pushed them both out of the way and walked right into the palace. The hall was huge with the king's throne on an elevated platform, along with many other chairs, on either side of the hallway. The king looked shocked after seeing us, he got up from his throne and said, "Who let you in?" Aetios stepped up and said in an intimidating voice, "There is no time for this right now, your city is in danger. Athenian soldiers are getting closer to the city." The king replied, "Don't make a mockery of this esteemed hall, do you think war is a joke?" Aetios knew the horrible pain of losing someone close to them, it is what war is all about. War is all about the loss of people, things, and places close to someone's heart. The king wouldn't listen but Aetios knew if they could not stop them, Lamia would fall.

Chapter 2

THE TWO-SIDED THREAT

The king did not want to believe Aetios, he was not ready for any kind of ambush. The king got a little worried, he sent one of the guards to the watchtower. It was just beside the hall, and was used mainly to watch over the whole city. Atreus said, “Why would not you believe us, we have no intention of lying to you.” The king was silent and just waited for the guard to return. The awkward silent came to an end when the guard came running down the hall, got onto his knees, and said, “They are coming, not only from the north gate, but the west gate is also getting ambushed.” The king’s face changed instantly like he had seen a ghost. He quickly ordered all his men to gather up and reinforce the gates. Aetios interrupted him and said, “We can help you, trust us.” “What can you little brats do in a war.” Aetios said in a low but resolute voice, “We can fight” as he drew his spear out. The king was startled by the sheer might of his words, he said, "Alright, do what you have to, but please don't let my city fall." Aetios was looking directly into his eyes, the thrust was increasing as every word came out of his mouth, and everybody stuck to the ground as Aetios moved, the thrust started decreasing and the atmosphere was lighter. Nobody could understand what had happened, but they could certainly feel it. Aetios ordered, "Eivor and Atreus will go to the west gate while me and Nathan will assist Percy on the north one." They parted ways and Aetios was looking more focused than ever.

THE WEST GATE

Eivor and Atreus were advancing towards the west gate, but the situation was not looking great. The streets were empty now, no one was seen, not even a single soul, except Eivor could see some. As they were about to approach the gate, they saw Spartan soldiers trying to hold them but loud noises were coming from the outer area. Eivor said, "What's going on?" Atreus quickly said, "I will check" as he fired an arrow with a rope tied at its tip. He used the rope to climb up the wall, and he saw a never-ending army of Athenians, trying to barge through the doors of the city, while the soldiers on top of the wall shot them with their arrows, it was a very chaotic situation, Atreus also started helping them, but to his astonishment the Athenians released a double-sided blade with a circular wooden base. Atreus had never seen such a thing. The blades started breaking through the wooden gates. He quickly looked down on the other side and shouted to Eivor, "They are here." He looked down as he had a purple hue around him, he was ready to fight anything and everything which came in his way. The doors were finally breached, the city was in danger of falling, and the only thing that stood in their way was the Spartan army and the soul-keeper. The Athenians started charging and got in front of the wooden oval machine, which Eivor was also surprised to see. Atreus was looking down from the high wall, he was trying his level best to help Eivor, but he was just standing there doing nothing, he hadn't even got his sword out. The Spartans also charged towards them, swords started clashing, bodies falling and blood spilling everywhere. They were killing each other, all the Spartans were killed, and the ones who were left were a group of Athenian soldiers. One of them asked in a creepy voice, "Oh, so you don't want to live, do you?" As soon as he said those words, Eivor started laughing like a psychopath, pulled out his sword, and struck it on the ground very softly. One by one the heads of those soldiers started falling off their bodies, but he wasn't even touching them. It was not possible to do such a thing. Atreus looking from above spotted a purple aura around the fallen Athenians. He knew it was the work of the souls, but how did he summon so many that fast? As Atreus was thinking about it, the circular blades started spinning in towards Eivor. Atreus tried to shoot it but it would not even make a scratch. Eivor tried to slow it down but the souls could not help him anymore, he looked exhausted. Atreus was worried but not blinded, he jumped off the wall while holding the rope and landed on the side of the circular bowl, it lost its balance. The blades rubbed against the land and were destroyed in the act, as the dust settled Eivor could see Atreus standing on it, wiping his shoulder. Atreus jumped down and said, "That was easier than I thought. But how did you summon so many souls?" Eivor replied in a low voice, "I just waited for them to get killed and later used their souls." Atreus was kind of scared by the fact that Eivor did not even think for a second before letting them all die. Atreus said as he looked towards the sky, "I wonder what might be taking place on the other side."

THE NORTH GATE

Aetios and Nathan were galloping towards the north gate, he was pretty worried about Percy. Aetios knew he was reckless, he had to be looked after, until he learn to control his anger. As they reached the gates, all the guards were standing there with heads hung down and no emotions on their faces. One of them approached Aetios and asked, "What is your friend doing?" Aetios and Nathan were clueless, they ran up the stairs. Aetios saw the enormous Athenian army standing on the other side of the bridge which was built over a river. As he looked down towards the entrance, he saw Percy sitting with his legs crossed in front of the gate and his sword stuck in the ground next to him. Aetios asked the archer next to him, "What's he been doing?" He replied calmly, "Absolutely nothing." Aetios was not surprised at all, that man had no sense of fear, he could be standing on the brink of death and still have an emotionless face. Both armies were ready to attack but no one was making the first move. The Spartans had the high-ground advantage but Athenians had something that could change the course of the war at its head. After some time, the Spartans heard, the general of the Athenian army shout, "ATTACK." The cavalry started charging on to the bridge, as they were about to cross the bridge Percy stood up and pulled his sword out of the ground, and a large wave of fire diverged from the place he was sitting on. The soldiers were knocked off their horses and some fell into the river too. Percy rushed towards the bridge as he wanted to kill every single soldier with his sword. The Athenians were not about to quit so easily, they released a monster from the back of the army, Nathan got shocked after seeing such a creature. It was a giant two headed snake. He had never seen such a thing. Percy was already fighting the army so the snake had clear ground to attack the gates. Aetios had to react quickly, so he pulled his spear out and launched it towards the two-headed monster. He pinned one of its heads to the ground. Nathan observed a green smoke coming out of its severed head. The Athenians who were fighting Percy also started running away. No one could understand anything but Percy started coughing heavily and fell to the ground, he was closest to the gas. Aetios opened his hand and asked, "What is happening?" as the spear flew into his hand. A familiar voice said, "The army was just a distraction, the snake was meant to be killed." Everyone expect Aetios turned around and were shocked. He said, "So you finally decided to come." Vulcan was standing there with red and white robes, a long beard, and a not-so-happy face. He continued, "We have to save that brat." A guard interrupted him and said, "What could a drunkard like you do in a battle." Aetios said in a gentle voice, "So, you haven't told anyone, have you?" He replied, "You know I am tired of these things" as he raised his arms, the water from the river started rising, a giant bubble of water formed above the bridge with some Athenian soldiers in the bubble. He swept his arms across and the water settled down the gas. Everyone was shocked except Aetios, he was smiling like never before. Nathan was out of words, "Bu- but h- ho- how did you do that?" Vulcan said, "Oh don't bother yourself with the details, just know me and the four elements have a good understanding." The Spartans had mixed feelings as they had just seen their city get saved by an old drunkard. The poisonous gas could have affected many people if it wasn't stopped outside the gates. Eivor and Atreus also arrived just after, Eivor was in a hurry to meet Vulcan, and he inquired, "Hey! why didn't you open your door when we were there?" Vulcan looked closely at Eivor and whispered, this aura is as dark as a starless sky. The others didn't hear it but Eivor went on to say, "So how did you win?" Nathan replied, "Vulcan helped us." Eivor couldn't believe it, "What? This guy, I thought he could barely walk." Vulcan was slowly losing his temper. Aetios knew it, so he instantly changed the topic, "I think we should check on Percy." We all went downstairs where Percy was being treated by the royal medics. Vulcan got there and said, "Get aside." He pulled all the poison out of his body and put it in a pouch hanging on his belt. Percy instantly opened his eyes, he saw Vulcan bended over him. He jumped up and said, "What are you doing here, you freak?" "Oh don't worry, I just saved your precious pride." Vulcan knew something about the weapons but Aetios knew he was not a persuasive man. It would take a lot to get something from him.

Chapter 3

WHATEVER IT TAKES

Vulcan was leading the group but was not talking at all, Aetios felt like he had come up with some topic, so he said, “Hey Vulcan, I heard some people saying you are a blacksmith now.” He did not even turn but luckily answered, “Yes, after your father’s death I had no intention of helping Sparta. The only thing I had interest in was forging.” He again went dead silent, but Aetios did not give up. When they reached his house, he started checking out the armor and weapons he had made. Vulcan didn’t know the meaning of hospitality, he just shouted at Aetios and told him to sit down at the table. His house was very congested, with a round table in the middle, his forging station in a corner, and weapons hanging everywhere. All of them sat around the table where swords were laid in front of every chair, converging in the center. There were a total of twelve chairs, Percy was quick to start the conversation, “You know why we are here, right?" "I know you are here to seek answers but I don't understand what do you need answers for." Eivor said swiftly, "Do you know about the Prophecy?" Vulcan rolled his eyes up and said, "Do I… of course, I know about the prophecy." As he said it, Aetios pulled out his spear and placed it on the table. Vulcan was amazed, he couldn't stop admiring the beauty of that occult spear. He said, "So, you've found the first one. I see. But do you know what this weapon is capable of?" Aetios was a bit confused as he had seen its powers but wasn't sure that those were the only ones. Aetios asked, "What powers are you talking about?" "I am not the right person to teach you about the might of this dangerous weapon. But, do you know your path ahead?" Nathan replied sarcastically, "Yeah, about that. We were wondering if you knew what other weapons are out there." He got up from his seat and started looking through the cabinet of his ancient books, he pulled out a leather-covered book which was falling apart but was still quite readable. He opened it on a page which had a weird-looking symbol, Aetios quickly remembered it from the time he saw it on one of the thrones during the meeting with the Pythia. Aetios quickly asked, "What is that symbol?" "Oh, I am glad that you asked. This is the symbol… of darkness, this is the symbol of HADES." All of the boys looked at Eivor as he was also in awe. Eivor said in a low voice, "But what does this have to do with the weapons." Vulcan replied, "Legend tells a tale of two great relics held by the god of the underworld, the Helm of Darkness and the mighty Blades of Hades. These blades possess the twilight of every single human and monster's soul. It is said that they could entrap the soul of the person killed by them." Nathan asked hurridly, "But the question is where are they now?" "The book says that these blades were forged in the depths of Hades, in Tartarus, and were dipped in each of the five rivers, surrounding the underworld. They are in Tarturus where Kronos lives." Atreus said, "Yes I have heard about him, Kronos used to eat his kids alive on birth, but Zeus escaped and decided to take revenge on him in the great Titan war where the Olympians overthrew their reign and captured Mount Olympus." Vulcan was quite impressed by their knowledge of Olympian Gods. Nathan said doubtfully, "But, I don't think anyone knows the entrance to Hades." Vulcan again turned to get a book but this time it had the symbol of a staff surrounded by two snakes and also had two wings at its tip. He read out the first page:

"The underworld is not a place to travel, to go there is the end of one's life. The souls of the deceased go to different parts of the underworld depending on their deeds. There was one God who led the souls to the entrance of Hades. He was the quickest and the cleverest of them all, the messenger of the gods, Hermes."

Eivor was very confused, he could not understand who Hermes was. He asked out of curiosity, "Hermes? That name doesn't ring a bell." Vulcan giggled a bit and said, "The Pythia must have told you, that you are not the only ones with godly potential, there are seven others with the abilities of Gods. You will need to find the Reincarnation of Hermes. That is your only hope to reach the underworld." Aetios said, "But, how are we supposed to find him, we don't know what he looks like." "You will know when you will see him, his aura will be different from others. He will feel different." Everyone sighed and agreed. They were in for one adventurous ride. Eivor questioned, "What about the other one, the Helm." Vulcan was silent for a moment and it was as if he had to gather some confidence up and spoke, "The Helm, you ask? Come let's go on a little walk, everyone else remains here." Vulcan took Eivor out of the cottage and towards the open fields. Vulcan started by saying, "Look, Eivor you have a very different personality and aura than all the others. You need to control your powers quickly, or else they could harm your body." Eivor understood the risk and asked, "I know I can talk to souls but I can only see them involuntarily. Moreover, I don't even know what other powers I have." Vulcan had something planned in his mind and knew that Eivor would need some encouragement. He said as he tapped the light blue crystal hanging from his neck, "I want to show you something." Eivor and Vulcan instantly teleported from the spot, they landed on top of a mountain, Eivor felt quite dizzy, it was his first time. Vulcan continued as he pointed at a large-scale war going on at the foot of the mountain, "Look down there, that is the great Titan war. Zeus, Poseidon, and Hades fought together to stop the Titans. Hades had a rather unique ability, he was not seen throughout the war but was heavily involved in it. He was granted the power of invisibility by the Helm of Darkness. He was destroying the army, but he was not just handed over the Helm. He was a very brave and clever God. The Cyclopes of Mount Etna gave it to him for his greatness." Eivor was impressed and wanted to get that relic, "Where can I find that Helm?" "The Helm is said to appear to a person who is clever enough to succeed Hades. I know, the Helm will appear to you, I have seen your potential but you have to use it to the fullest. You are the soul keeper, you don't just see souls, you command them, all of them." He again touched his crystal and they teleported in front of the cottage. You need not to tell anyone else. They entered the house and saw Aetios and the others sleeping. Vulcan said, "I think you should also take some rest, it has been a tiring day." Eivor agreed but said, "Don't you want to sleep?" "No, I don't sleep." Eivor was quick to question him again, "But why?" Vulcan replied in a soft voice, "Now that is a story for another time." Nobody was lucky enough to hear Vulcan talk softly. Vulcan had grown a unique affection for Eivor. He related to him, Vulcan was a very powerful sorcerer, he could control all four elements but he was also consumed by the hunger of wanting more. Our heroes would now have to find the reincarnation of Hermes, which was a very hard task in itself. They have no clue where to even start but who knows what a new day might bring.

Chapter 4

THE DREAMING CITY

The next morning Aetios and Percy woke up first, and they got out of the house. Cool wind was blowing continuously and the Sun was still nowhere to be seen. Percy said, "The weather is getting colder day by day." Aetios agreed and said as he looked up into the cloudy sky, "What do you think Vulcan told him yesterday." Percy didn't know but he said, "Vulcan is an intelligent man, despite all his stubbornness he is still very nice at heart." Aetios and Percy started grooming their horses when Vulcan came up from behind, he stood still and was silent. He went inside and woke everyone else up. They were ready to leave Lamia at last, but they had no clue about their next destination. Aetios whispered to Vulcan, "Where should we go now?" Vulcan took a long breath and said, "There is a city not far west from here, Loutra Ypatis. A friend of mine lives there, his name is Herodotus. He might be able to help you find the reincarnation of Hermes." Aetios had never heard of that city but he believed his old friend." They started riding west, not knowing what awaited them in that city.

After three hours, riding felt easier than before, the colder weather was a better experience than the scorching hot Sun. They could now see the entrance of that city in the distance. It looked distinctive. Aetios could feel something unusual but didn't understand it. They reached the gate and to their surprise, no guard was standing there. Eivor got off his horse and opened the gate. The city was dead quiet, no person could be seen anywhere. It was almost like no one lived there. Everyone else got off their horses and were surprised, they could not comprehend anything. Percy said in a whispering voice, "We should split up and look for someone who could help us." Atreus was not so sure about this idea, he did not like going alone in eerie places. The frightening solitude was scaring everyone inside but they had to find someone to talk to. Everyone split up.

Percy went towards the dwellings, they looked like they had never been open. Every single house was covered with wild grass, he tried opening a door but it was stuck. Percy kicked the door and entered the house. He was surprised by what he saw, a man, a woman, and a child lying on the bed. He got near to check them, Percy thought they were dead but they were still breathing. Percy said to himself, "Are they sleeping?" He could not figure out why were they sleeping in a destroyed house. He quickly ran to check the other houses. One after another, every door he opened he saw, people sleeping, some lying on floors and some hanging onto furniture. He was confused. The atmosphere was becoming more intense every minute. It was like they were sleeping for quite some time now.

Eivor went the other way towards the fields of that city, where crops were dead due to lack of water and the ground had cracks in it. Eivor suspected that the city must have experienced a drought in the past. He checked everywhere but could not find anyone to talk to, or did he? He found a soul just wandering on the other side of those fields. It was an old man with a large grey mustache, and steel rimmed glasses, he was wearing a long black robe but was barefoot. Eivor waved at him and asked, "Hey old man, what are you doing here?" The old man had a frowning look on his face, he said, "I should ask you the same question. These are my fields, I looked after the crops when I was alive." Eivor was bored, so he asked the man, "So tell me, how did you die?" The old man replied, "Why should I tell you?" Eivor looked directly into his eyes, purple glow surrounded his pupil. The old man spoke once more, "I was just looking after my crops when a tall man, had a helmet on, a brown colored vest, and a necklace came up to me, and pulled out his sword. I was scared so I ran towards the city, he did not follow me. When I entered my house I saw everyone sleeping. I quickly checked the other houses but they were also in deep sleep. I didn't know what to do, suddenly the same man appeared again, out of nowhere. He had a small grin on his face and said, "You are not so lucky, are you?" as he cut my body in half." Eivor could not believe it, somebody so cruel to split a living man in half. He had quite some information but still did not know how everyone fell asleep.

Nathan went towards the market place of Loutra Ypatis. Atreus was too scared to go alone, so he followed him. Surprisingly, the market was open, but, it was grim. Everything was covered in dust, the vendors were sleeping in their shops. Atreus was confused but Nathan had an idea of what was happening. He said in a low voice, "I think I know what's going on here. I have read a tale about the dreaming city, but I thought it was just a story." Atreus became curious and asked, "What else do you know about it?" Nathan looked down the road and said, "It is said this city is possessed by a demon, who put all these people to sleep. The curse can only break if the demon is killed." Atreus was a bit confused now, "But who would bring the demon here?" Nathan sighed and said, "Most probably, the evil one."

Aetios went to the king's palace situated on the highest point in the city. He did not know what he was in for. The gates were already open with no guards present. Aetios was already suspicious. He was ready to defend himself if anything came his way. He entered the palace but it was all empty. He thought everybody would be in the throne room. He was right but they were all unconscious. The hall was looking very wild, tree branches had grown out of the ground and a very foul smell was present in the hall. Aetios approached the king, he was still breathing but was in very ugly shape. His beard was fully grown out, his robes were dirty and he was looking very weak. Aetios could sense an unusual presence in that hall, it was a very negative energy. Aetios did not feel good, he drew his spear out, and he heard something rustling behind him. He quickly turned around and saw a black tentacle trying to grab him, he stabbed it and pinched it to the ground. He was not confident enough to fight something like that alone, so he returned to the place where they split up.

Percy was already sitting there with Nathan and Atreus joined shortly after. Nathan asked Percy, "What did you find?" Percy was silently sitting on a rock. He got up and said, "I think you guys also found the same thing as I did." Atreus was scared, he nodded. Eivor also came running in and said, "Oh! so you guys are already here, I found an old man, he was killed by a swordsman." Percy was very suspicious but waited for Aetios to arrive. Aetios slowly walked, thinking about the tentacle that attacked him. Percy shouted from a distance, "Hurry up, will you?" Aetios quickly came up to them and asked, "What did you guys find?" Percy again said angrily, "It doesn't matter what we found, what have you got?" Aetios was not so sure why Percy was so angry all of a sudden. He said, "I searched the castle and found everyone sleeping." Nathan said, "That's what we all found." Aetios replied, "But I found something else too." Eivor was suspicious and interrupted him, "Was it a tall man." Aetios sighed and said, "No it was not human, it attacked me with a tentacle. It had a unique presence, a negative one." As Aetios was saying this the clouds gathered up, everyone disappeared and he was standing on a cliff. Looking down he saw the evil one destroying a city. He looked closely and noticed that the city was Athens. He was followed by five more black-cloaked individuals who were riding chariots with black horses in front of them. They were a menace, Athens was beyond saving. Aetios was very worried but he knew it was just a past vision after seeing such destruction, he got a small glimpse of the evil one's powers. Suddenly everyone was back, Aetios was petrified by the vision he just saw. Nathan said, "I told Atreus about it, we can free this city of its curse by killing that monster." Percy got up and said, "So what are we waiting for, let's go and save the city." Aetios liked Percy's confidence but was very concerned about Deimos's growing power. He knew they needed to move quickly and find the reincarnation of Hermes. They thought they knew everything about the evil one but there was more about him than what came in front of one's eyes.

Chapter 5

SOLARIS, THE GOLDEN KNIGHT

Percy insisted on going into the palace to fight the monster but Aetios knew they had to devise a plan first or else they would not survive. He said, “We don’t know anything about its strength or weakness. We don’t even know its location. We will slowly work our way through the castle and find it first.”

Everyone followed Aetios to the castle, they entered the gates, it was as silent as a graveyard. They could hear the wind. Percy had been patient long enough, he said, “Just follow me, I am going to find that beast and slay it myself.” Everybody believed in Percy but the spooky environment got them all scared. They walked into the throne room where Aetios had been earlier. Aetios could still sense the negative emotions but no one else could. Nathan asked Aetios, “Can you still sense its presence?”

Aetios nodded in agreement. Nathan continued, "We need you to lead us to it, only you can do that because none of us can sense." Aetios closed his eyes and concentrated on that adverse emotion, he sensed it being further down the castle. Aetios assumed it might be in the dungeons under the castle. Aetios said, "We need to go down to the dungeons." Atreus was scared again, he was always scared of creepy places.

They reached the old wooden gates of the dungeons, they were slightly open. Percy stepped through and saw a woman suspended in air with tentacles coming out of her spine but the thing that surprised Percy the most was that she was unconscious. All of them entered the grim place with broken pillars everywhere and very little light to see anything. Aetios quickly signaled everyone to stand in a defensive stance. The tentacles started attacking them from every single direction. Each one they cut down grew back even longer than before. It was a total mess. Percy was slashing down every single one of them which just made their situation even worse. Aetios shouted, "Don't cut them off, just don't get caught." Now that was not an easy task to escape so many slimy tentacles attacking you. One by one everyone got caught by them. Everyone was wrapped by the tentacles and rendered unconscious. Aetios was the only one left. He grabbed Hofund from Percy's hand and knew what he had to do. He tapped the tip of the sword and all of a sudden he had the Golden red armor surrounding him with the helm of the Wolf. He was feeling more confident than before, Percy changed his spear's mode and started slamming the tentacles down to the ground, this way it would not chop them off thus resulting in no newer ones. He was making some progress but the wolf mode had started exhausting Aetios, he was feeling very tired. He knelt and the armor disappeared. His eyes were slowly closing as at least twenty tentacles reached for him. As he was about to pass out, he heard a rather sweet voice say, "LIGHT VOID." He could not bear to turn around and see who it was. He finally fell to the ground unconscious not knowing what happened.

Three hours had passed, and Aetios' eyes slowly reopened, he saw a camp fire and sitting beside it a tall, handsome man with long golden brown hair, a sporty physique, and a blindfold on his eyes. He turned his head towards Aetios and said in a familiar voice, "Oh, so you are finally awake." He extended his hand forward, "My name is Solaris." Aetios was shaken by the pure beauty of that voice and shook his hand as he was still admiring his looks. Aetios quickly snapped out of it and asked, "Where is everyone else?" Solaris pointed toward the still-unconscious Percy, Nathan, Eivor, and Atreus and said, "They are still under the effect of the curse." Aetios looked confused, they had killed the monster.

Solaris understood those expressions and said, "The curse will lift in the moonlight and there are still three hours remaining for that. Morpheus was just a pawn set by one of Deimos' generals. They are trying to slow you down." Aetios was getting more confused after every word he said. How did he know about their mission? He had so many questions. He said, "How do you know about us? How did you find us?" Solaris giggled a bit and said, "I knew about you when I was a teenager, I had read the prophecy and have been trying to find you ever since. I was told by a man named Theseus that you would be here." Aetios had a smile on his face as he thought about him, he was still watching over them, "Still, what role do you have to play in this, an ordinary man cannot destroy a creature with one single attack." Solaris got up and said in a low but resolute voice, "I have the powers of Apollo. I can control light." Aetios could not believe his eyes. They were not even trying to find him, but nature has a way of surprising everyone. They waited for the Moon to shine, everyone slowly woke up, Percy and the others were very dizzy at first but as soon as they saw Solaris, astonishment covered their faces. They were awestruck by his sheer beauty. Percy asked, "What happened?" Aetios replied in a rush, "You all were also cursed and I was also about to faint when Solaris killed the creature with one attack." Atreus was the most impressed by the fact that he only used one single attack. Nathan said, "We have to find

Herodotus." Aetios and the others had almost forgotten about their main motive for coming to Loutra Ypatis. Solaris was very confused, he did not know about any of this. He asked, "Who is that guy?" They were not very keen on retelling the whole Battle of Lamia and then telling him about Vulcan so, Aetios just said, "He is the one who might know something about the reincarnation of Hermes." Solaris had a unique smile on his face and said in a proud voice, "Why exactly do we need him?" He was truly confused as they had not told him anything about the blades. Percy was still a bit suspicious of him, but Aetios said, "Only he can take us to the underworld to find the Blades of Hades." Solaris now understood some parts and said, "Let me guess, He is the one with the powers of Hades" as he pointed towards Eivor. Everyone was a bit surprised, Nathan asked in an astonished voice, "But how do you know about it?" Solaris replied, "Oh, I can sense all your auras." Everyone listened to him carefully as he explained the mystery of auras, "Aura is the direct representation of a person's personality. Every single one of you can sense auras too but you need some experience first. I can see and tell everyone's aura." He pointed towards Percy and said, "This one has a bright orangey-red aura just like the flames of Ares. I think we should go and meet Herodotus as quickly as possible." Everyone agreed. They got on their horses but Solaris had no horse, he sat behind Aetios. Percy was even more suspicious now, if he had no horse how did he get here? He ignored it for now but started keeping a close eye on him.

They rode down towards the city and asked people for Herodotus, they said he would be in a two-story house near the well. They quickly rode towards the well and saw a wide brick house with a dull grey door and a brown horse tied outside it. Everyone got off their horses and stood in front of the gate, Aetios knocked but no one answered for a while. He knocked once again but still no one answered. He tried to push it and surprisingly it was already open. They all slowly walked in. The walls and floor were as clean as a whistle. It was beautifully built. They shouted "HERODOTUS." They walked into a library, where thousands of books were placed in wooden racks. It was not the best of the sights for Eivor's eyes as he hated books. He had a frown on his face. A middle-aged man was standing in blue and white robes with a hood at his back. Solaris touched his shoulder and his head slowly turned. He instantly jumped in astonishment and said, "Oh! heavens above. Who are you?" He had a unique voice, it was low but heavy. Aetios stepped forth and said, "Vulcan has sent us here." He had reassurance on his face as he said, "You should have told me before. It would have been much easier for me." Percy said in a stern voice, "Do you know where to find the reincarnation of Hermes." His face was suddenly very neutral. He put his head down and said, "No I don't know about him, you can go now." Aetios observed that he was suspicious of them and did not want to disclose anything. He pulled out his spear and slammed it on the ground. Herodotus suddenly saw the spear and could not take his eyes off it. Percy said, "So, will you tell us now?" He replied, "His name is Angelos, he was here about three days ago." Everyone was shocked, Atreus asked curiously, "What does he look like?" "He is a young lad with blonde hair and is very clever. He stole many things while he stayed in Loutra Ypatis." Aetios knew it was their best chance to get near him, he asked, "Do you know where he was going after leaving this city?" Herodotus nodded and said, "He was going to Delphi to take part in the Olympic games." Solaris' face lit up as he said, "We should go there right away, I know many people there." Everyone agreed, they left the house and were ready to ride, when Herodotus said, "The games start this morning, I hope you know about that." Everyone was disgusted, he could have told them earlier. Nathan said, "It is not possible to make it in one night." Solaris chuckled and said, "Oh you don't even know what is possible." He joined his hands to make a weird symbol and murmured something, in an instant there stood a gold and white chariot driven by two pure white horses. Everyone was awestruck, how could he do that? There was more to Solaris than just met the eye. Atreus asked, "How did you do that?" Solaris replied, "This is a summon, every God had one. You guys have a lot more to learn than I thought." As impressive as it was, they had to focus on finding Angelos to get the Blades of Hades.

Chapter 6

NO GUTS, NO GLORY

Everybody was on the chariot, ready for the horses to start galloping through the woods but when the horses started running, the chariot was in the air. It was flying high above the forest. Solaris looked at Aetios, winked, and said, “I told you, you have a lot to learn.” Atreus was very curious about how summons work. He said, “Still you should tell us how these things work, please teach us.” Solaris was very friendly to all of them, he said, “It is not something learned in one night, but to summon your spirit animal you needs to be one with your soul. Your concentration power should be at its peak. You need to befriend your summon to use its full capabilities.” He pointed at the horses and said, “Corus and Aether are very loyal. They are the horses of Apollo.” The Sun was starting to rise and they were closing in on Delphi. The city was a huge maze, one could get lost very easily. It had huge temples and statues of different Gods. The city was looking very crowded from the chariot as a lot of people had come to see The Olympic Games. As they were about to land on the ground, Aetios suddenly felt an extremely severe headache, he had a vision again.

He saw a very dark room, with an extensively long table. As he tried to focus his sight, he saw two deep green eyes staring at him. As he moved closer he saw something that shook his body from head to toe. Deimos sitting on the end of the table with the scythe in his hand and was looking furious, his bloodthirsty eyes wanting revenge. Five other people stood there who were supposedly listening to his orders. He looked in the direction Aetios was standing, he got startled, "Can he see me?"

As he said those words he was back at Delphi, with Solaris and Nathan standing over him. He quickly got up and said, "Where are Percy, Eivor and Atreus? Nobody should see us here. Deimos, he's here, in Delphi. If he knows we are here too, he will try to kill us all." Solaris' eyes widened and he said, "The evil one? What is he doing here." "I could not care less but I know that we have to stay undetected, no one should know our true identity." Nathan looked a bit confused and said, "B… but they are already gone." Aetios' gestures changed from concerning to raging red, he was absolutely vexed,

"What? Where did they go? We have to find them now. Let's split up, but keep one thing in your mind, do not draw any kind of attention."

They all split up, Solaris went east in search of one of the three, he was still thinking about, the Evil One. Everyone in all the lands were scared to even say his name, the thought of being near him was a terrifying one. Solaris was very experienced and knew the potential of his powers, unlike the whole team who were just getting into it. He went towards the huge stadium with flags hoisted outside it and loud noises could be heard over vast distances. He entered the stadium through a gateway where stood a boy offering little pieces of paper that read:

"Come and join me in paradise."

Solaris grinned and said, "What is that supposed to mean?" The boy was looking very petrified and said, "I do not know anything, I was just paid to distribute these." Solaris said, "Whatever" and continued into the arena. He sat on the stairs with all the other locals. They were all excited for what was to come. He leaned over and asked a man sitting next to him with dirty robes and a heavy mustache, "What is happening here?" He was surprised to see Solaris. He thought to himself, 'who wears a blindfold around the eyes? How can he see?' he asked, "Are you blind?" Solaris chuckled and said, "No. These eyes are too precious to be seen by everyone." The guy said, "Someone is about to get destroyed by the Nemean Beast." Solaris had a moment of realization, he could only think of one creature from Nemean. As he was thinking a bold voice said, "Get ready, everyone. Whether you have come from a far or you live in this alluring city, you will be entertained by this fight before the Olympics begin. Here I present to you, our first warrior, Elpenor, the witful." As the gates on one side of the arena opened, he saw a tall man walk out, he had a sword and a shield in his hand. He wore green robes with a leather armor. He looked confident. As he reached the middle of the arena waving to the crowd, the bold voice spoke again, "Unleash the beast." The atmosphere was already starting to get tense, people started cheering, as if they wanted to see bloodshed. The gates were slowly opening on the other end, but the beast didn't wait. He smashed past them and everyone saw a lion but he was double the size of any other. He growled loudly, the people stopped cheering for a moment but then cheered even louder again. The bold voice said again, "BEGIN." Elpenor slowly started moving sideways, in a defensive stance. The lion was looking as proud as it should be, he waited for the swordsman to attack. As soon as Elepenor attacked, he slapped him with his paw. After seeing the swordsman fall, he pounced on him and ripped him apart as blood spilled everywhere. Solaris was quite bored and was about to leave when the bold voice spoke once again, "Up next is a young warrior from Sparta, Percy, The Fireheart." Solaris' breath stopped for a moment. He could not believe what was about to happen. Solaris had never seen Percy's abilities, he was a bit too curious about him, and his aura amazed The Golden Knight. Percy stepped onto the arena, looking fresh and focused as always. Anyone who knew Percy could have guessed him being here. He had Hofund on his shoulder, with no shield. Percy always fought without a shield as he thought it was just useless if you knew how to defend yourself properly. He stood in the middle of the arena staring into the bloodthirsty eyes of the Nemean Beast. The unbreakable confidence of Percy was on full display as the crowd sat in complete and utter silence. The obscure presence of the young warrior was flying over everyone's head except Solaris who sat back down with his legs crossed elegantly. A guy sitting next to him said, "This one is also going to die, the same way Elpenor did." Solaris chuckled and said, "Oh, this one is different. Just watch." Percy gripped Hofund with both his hands, put one foot forward, and was ready for any attack that was thrown his way. The lion pounced on him, but Percy barely rolled out of his way and tried to strike him with his sword but to his sudden surprise it did not even cut his skin. Percy knew the odds were against him but he still had a cold smile on his candid face. He tried again and again but failed miserably every single time. He knew the sword would not work on him, so he rolled the sword around his wrist, the sword facing downwards he struck it into the ground and got ready to fight barehanded as he put up his hands towards his chest and shook them convulsively. Everyone in the crowd was confused at this sight. A young kid was going to fight the Nemean Lion without any weapon. Solaris thought, 'Now, that's a bold move. Even I wouldn't try and do that.' Percy was serious, he thought of it as the only way to beat the wild beast. Percy started running to get behind him but the lion jumped and moved around in circles to avoid it. The tension was growing higher every second, the crowd started cheering. Percy knew he had to make a move quickly. Solaris' eyes deviated from the fight and fell on an attractive, fine blue-eyed young girl with blonde hair. She was one of the most exquisite girls in the world. She was wearing a bright pink dress which complimented the beauty of her rosy cheeks. She was sitting next to the King of Delphi. She looked concerned about the fight. She didn't even flinch when Elpenor died. While he was looking away the lion tried to hit Percy with his paw which had a direct hit on him. The princess stood up in shock but Solaris knew what was coming. All this time whenever Percy fell he got up even stronger, he sometimes got really out of control. Once again Percy got up, his eyes turned orangey red, and his aura started glowing. All of a sudden he teleported beside the lion. The guy sitting in the audience asked, "What happened there?" Solaris said in a sarcastic voice, "He is too fast for your eyes."

Percy punched his stomach, The lion fell to the ground. He was furious, as he opened his mouth Percy could see its extremely sharp teeth, but he still had no grin on his face. As soon as he was about to eat him alive, Percy grabbed both sides of his abruptly large mouth. Everyone in the stadium was shocked by the sheer power of Percy, their jaws dropped. Although Solaris was still not impressed, he believed that he had much more potential in him. He suddenly started screaming and waves of fire spread all across the stadium, putting cracks in the walls. Everybody had to cover themselves from the horrific incoming fire. Solaris said in a low voice, "Now that's some heat." As Percy was screaming he started pushing the lion's mouth the opposite way and ripped it apart. Blood splattered everywhere. The crowd went mad and started running out of the stadium, the pure wrath of Percy's power was enough to scare a whole nation. The king and princess also stood up, Percy turned around, and looked her dead in the eyes and fell to the ground instantly. Solaris rushed into the arena, grabbed Percy, put him on his shoulder, and whistled for his chariot. He flew right out of the stadium to get Percy treated, on the other hand he could not figure out the mystery of Percy and the Princess of Delphi.

Chapter 7

MASTER OF PUPPETS

Aetios was still roaming around the city looking for everyone, not knowing what had occurred on the other side of this beautiful city. He was roaming around and saw a suspicious-looking person who was silently staring at him. He was wearing a full black robe, and as soon as Aetios caught him staring he started running away. He shouted, "Hey! you, stop right there." But as expected he kept running, and Aetios had to chase him down. They turned around tight corners, jumped over quite a lot of shops, and then climbed up to the roof of the buildings surrounding them. They were leaping from one roof to another getting in the way of the locals who shouted at them. As they were running Aetios pulled out his spear, whispered something to it, and threw it towards the mysterious man. It hit one of his legs and he fell to the side into a courtyard of an empty house. Aetios jumped down and said, "You are quite a runner I will give you that." He took the spear out of his leg and uncovered his face, as the black hood was pulled off Aetios saw a bald man with a fair complexion. Everything about him was alright except his eyes, they were pitch black. There was nothing but darkness in those eyes. He spoke, "We meet once again Aetios." He was really confused and said, "Oh, we have met before, don't you remember? It was not the best of the meetings." Aetios slowly realized and said, "Oh! so I was right. You are in Delphi. What do you expect to find here?" "Oh, you are so naive, I will just warn you, there might be a glazed flame coming your way." "That explains why you have hijacked an innocent civilian's body. Why don't you face me yourself." Aetios was trying to provoke him as Deimos was short-tempered. "Let me tell you one thing, I don't like to get my hands dirty." As soon as he said that, a dart came and hit Aetios's neck. He held his throat pulled the dart out and said, "Oh, no." He fainted soon afterwards, as he saw the guy in front of him dissolve into the ground.

Atreus and Eivor were still darting around the city, they had little clue about what was happening. They were just walking through the beautiful streets of the city as they came across a huge open field with hundreds of people surrounding it. Confused at the strange sight, Eivor asked a person at the back end of the crowd, "What is happening here?" He turned around, looked at him suspiciously, and said, "Don't you know, it is the most anticipated event of the Olympics. The Race." Atreus and Eivor both looked at each other and thought this would be quite fun to watch. They started pushing through the crowd to get in front. They tried their best, they got pushed, stepped on, and even got some elbows to the face before reaching the front of the anticipating audience. As they barely made it to front, they saw the contestants warming up on the starting line. There were four participants, a lean, tall man with an Athenian vest and a blue headband, a short, black-haired woman, a rather unusual man with a wooden leg, and finally a young lad with white curly hair and golden boots. They were all stretching at the starting line ready to run the race of their lifetime. A pretty heavy man stepped beside them and started shouting, "Get ready, ladies and gentlemen for an event never held before in the history of The Olympics." Then he proceeded to start the race by producing a gong, as he hit the giant round, golden brown gong. Everyone ran like their life depended on it but the white-haired boy just stood there, biting his nails. They had to finish where they started, completing a whole lap of the field. The whole crowd was shouting and cheering for their favourite contestants, the Athenian warrior was in first place followed closely by the short lady. The guy with the wooden leg staggered behind all of them. They were about to complete their lap when the boy looked behind, he saw all the three participants coming so he smiled and suddenly vanished for a moment. Everyone started shouting as if they thought he was cheating but Atreus knew the truth. The boy had not vanished, his speed was too much for the naked human eye to comprehend, Atreus said, "No, Eivor. This boy is special, he did not vanish, he is running too fast." As they were talking, all the contestants suddenly fell to the ground. Eivor exclaimed, "What? What happened there?" Atreus had a keen eye on the situation and said, "It's him again, the boy. He went past them at top speed." "How can you even see that?" Atreus said, "I don't know, I just see it normally." The boy appeared on the finish line and everyone started cheering instantly. Atreus could not understand the randomness of such people. Eivor looked astonishingly at the speedster, Atreus said, "I have a suspicion, we might have found who we were looking for, but we will have to wait and see." He turned to Eivor and said, "Go find Aetios and the others, I will keep him occupied for the moment." Eivor nodded and quickly went on to find the team. Atreus backed off from the crowd and walked near the podiums where the medals were to be awarded. He just stood near pretending to be one of the soldiers. Every winner came near the podium, obviously, the boy with the first place, and following him were the dizzy runner-ups. He just stood there while they were being presented with tiaras made out of white flower petals and leaves. As the little boy came down from the podium, Atreus purposely bumped into him and said in a rather crooked and shrill voice, "Oh! I am sorry. Oh! my God, are you the boy who just won the race?" The little boy smiled and said in a light voice, "Yes, that was me." Atreus again acted like he was shocked, he covered his mouth with his hands, gasped loudly, and said, "Really? Can I know your name?" "My name is Angelos." Atreus was right about his identity, he quickly said, "I need to show you something you will love." Angelos nodded and they left the field.

Eivor was wandering around the city looking for the team. As he was lurking around he saw the massive energy surge created by Percy, standing in awe, he was speechless. He re-gathered himself and quickly started running towards it.

Solaris had flown Percy safely out of the arena. They were sitting outside on a huge rock. Percy was lying half conscious in the chariot. As Solaris got out of it, he saw the princess of Delphi running towards him with her boots in her hands and holding her dress up so she wouldn't trip. She immediately said in a sharp voice, "Where is he?" Solaris assumed she was talking about Percy and pointed towards the chariot. She was looking vexed. Solaris decided that it would be wise to stay out of this situation. Percy had just woken up and was still very dizzy. He turned his head and saw the princess just dashing towards him. His eyes opened wide and a flare of light appeared in his eyes. It was a gesture nobody had seen on Percy's face, Percy said, "Alessandra, what are you doing here?" She said in an angry voice, "I think I should be asking you the same question." Solaris was a bit confused by the situation but did not interfere. Percy replied, "I have some things to tell you. My life in these past couple of weeks has not been the same. I will tell you everything, just come with me. He got up, held her hand and they started walking away. Solaris stood in silence as if he wasn't even there. After a few minutes, Eivor comes running in, and says, "We found him, we found him!" Solaris turns around and says in a low voice, "It's about time."

Percy and Alessandra are walking in an empty street and he is trying to calm her down, "Look, my whole life was turned into a quest and expectations are high." Alessandra said, "Explain it." "I had just passed the army test when Theseus sent us on a mission to find some scroll, but little did I know that the scroll was about to change my life." Her expressions changed a bit and now she was curious, "But, what did the scroll say?" "It said that five warriors from Sparta were destined to find the five magical weapons of the Gods. The five warriors are me, Aetios, Eivor, Atreus, and Nathan." Alessandra was slowly returning to normal. “I would never do such a thing if it was not absolutely necessary.”

While Percy was trying his best to make Alessandra happy again, Solaris and Eivor found Atreus accompanied by the young blonde boy. As soon as Solaris saw the boy he quickly slashed his hand, a whip bolted out and cuffed both his hand and feet. “Not so fast, after all, who are you?” said Solaris mockingly. Atreus shouted, “Why are you doing that he is on our side.” “I know whose side he is on but I need to ensure what his motives are.” As Atreus was arguing with Solaris, he heard a rather echoed voice, “I think that’s not the biggest of your problems.” Solaris turned around and saw a man and a lady standing next to each other, wearing red and blue garments respectively. Solaris shouted back at them, “And who might you be?” The lady bent forward and said, “The Evil One sends his regards.” Eivor was furious and was about to charge at the distinctive duo when the one dressed in red, said, “You might want to reconsider that decision” as he raised his arm Aetios came floating to them but was unconscious. Everyone was outraged but they could not do anything. Angelos whispered to Solaris and said, “Just untie me, let me prove my loyalty” but Solaris did not answer. Atreus said, “What do you want?” They replied simultaneously, “Our master wants to see all of you dead, especially this one.” He pulled out a weird-looking staff and was about to cut

Aetios' head off. Solaris said in a low voice, "You better be right kid" as he snapped his fingers and Angelos got free. He smiled and all of a sudden disappeared, or as it seemed. He ran behind the duo, picked Aetios up, and got him back to Atreus and Eivor, seeing Aetios safe, Solaris put his right hand on the ground and a dome of light formed above him and the twins. Solaris said, "You are in my domain now" he opened the palm of his hand, and an Urumi with a blade made out of light appeared in his hand. An Urumi is like a flexible sword, more like a whip but in the shape of a sword. The environment was more intense than ever, Angelos had done his part and now it was onto Solaris to finish the job.

Chapter 8

A FORK IN THE ROAD

The blinding shine of the place was causing a problem for the evil duo but Solaris was unhinged by any of it. Solaris said, "Hey! you two just tell me your names." The man said loudly, "My name is Pyrrhus and my sister's name is Kari but why do you want to know our names?" He replied menacingly, "I have to write something on your gravestones when I bury you." Kari was really angry and flew into Solaris and it seemed like she crashed into Solaris. It looked like she had a clean shot on Solaris but when the smoke cleared Pyrrhus was shocked when he saw Kari kneeling to the ground and Solaris was sitting on her back. Solaris said mockingly, "I thought you two would attack together, this is disappointing." Kari flew once again and this time Pyrrhus flew too, they both flew right back in from opposite directions towards Solaris, it seemed like an undodgeable attack. Solaris just casually ducked down and both of them crashed into each other. Solaris giggled and said, "This is going to be easy." He slashed his Urumi along the ground and cut off the right arm of Pyrrhus. As soon as he did it, Kari tried to escape but flew right into the wall of light. Solaris said, "I am not going to kill you, yet." He snapped his fingers and the dome disappeared. Solaris turned around as the siblings ran away, he saw Percy and Alessandra running down towards Aetios. Percy quickly sat down with the still unconscious Aetios and said, "What happened, who did this?" Solaris said, "That is the wrong question, we should be looking for an injury that has done this." Alessandra walked in and said, "Let me see, I am learning healing techniques in the entire royal family, maybe I can do something." While she was checking Aetios, Atreus came up to Solaris and said, "You're sure we can trust that kid." Solaris smiled and said, "Don't worry, he's on our side, at least for now." Alessandra had completed her check and said, "He will be alright in a few hours, it is just a mild poison." As they were all talking, a man just appeared out of nowhere from above, landed straight down, and said, "Which one of you was it?" Eivor tried to see his face under the grey cloak that he had on, he was Vulcan. Nathan said, "What are you doing in Delphi?" "I don't want to leave Lamia but when I saw that power surge, I knew it was one of you kids." Alessandra stepped in and said, "Yes, it was Percy, I saw it with my own eyes. Nothing like I had ever seen before." Vulcan said with a little smirk on his face, "Of course, it was you. I need you to come with me." Percy was a bit confused, "But where?" "I will explain it on the way, if we don't act quickly, Deimos will not hold back. His power is growing as we speak, we need to train you to harness your power, if you let it loose it can hurt the ones you love." Percy glanced at Alessandra and said, "Let's go then" but she quickly grabbed his wrist, stopped him, and said if you are going somewhere I will go too, I will not let you do anything stupid anymore. Percy was a bit resistant and said, "But I don't want you to get hurt, the quest I am on is very dangerous. Death can meet me at any time." Alessandra said, "Then death will have to meet us together." Listening to this, Percy was a bit shaken and finally agreed to take Alessandra with him. Vulcan pushed his palm upwards and two horses made from rocks appeared. Vulcan got on the horse, Percy came over and whispered, "I think we might need one more horse." He smiled and replied, "I don't think you will kid. Apart from training you I might give you some advice or two about love too. Just help her onto the horse." Percy was really shy as he was not a person who knew the meaning of love. He did as Vulcan told him and helped Alessandra get onto the horse and then sat behind her. Percy bid farewell to everyone and looked with tears in his eyes towards the unconscious Aetios as they rode out of the city.

Nathan said, “So, now it's just us guys, anybody wants to talk about how we are going to get to the Underworld.” Solaris said, “Our new friend here, “Angelos should be able to tell us all about it.” Angelos looked nervous and said, “Yes, but I have only been there once and it was the most terrifying experience I have ever had. I went to the city of souls and had to meet Thanatos to take his permission.” Eivor was curious and said, “What do you mean?” “You can see souls, that others cannot. I can see them too, we both are associated with the underworld and our work in this prophecy is tied to the underworld. For a living person to go to the underworld, they have to meet Thanatos first and then I can take you all to the Gates of Hades.” Solaris was listening carefully and said, “Let's be smart about this one, if we just stay here while you are in the ‘City Of Souls’ it will be a total waste of time. First of all, where even is this City Of Souls?” Angelos sighed and said, “It is not a place on the map like your usual cities, it exists between time and space. One cannot just walk into this city, you can only go there if you have the powers of the underworld. I am an exception because it is tied to my work, you see.” Nathan was a bit frustrated that he couldn’t go to explore a new place, “So, what do we do?” Angelos explained further, “So, I don’t know everything but I think the Oracle of Delphi will be able to answer all the questions?” Nathan was not at all happy that Eivor was about to venture into a new place and he would be going only to the ones he had already been to. Solaris said, "So let's not waste any time, we will head off to see the Oracle and you guys just do your own thing, and get permission from the God Of Death. I would rather not experience such a thing." Solaris, Atreus, Nathan, and Aetios headed off to meet the Oracle while Eivor and Angelos attempted to enter the City Of Souls.

Eivor was a bit confused and said, "So, how exactly do we get to this city?" Angelos sat down with his legs crossed and said, "Just sit down with me, close your eyes, and try to sense your aura, try to recognize your soul, the soul of Hades." Eivor also sat down, closed his eyes, and started deep breathing. He tried to sense his aura, he could do it but it was strange as he had never felt like this. He had never focused hard enough to sense anyone's aura let alone his own. He started seeing a purple light getting brighter and brighter. In a few seconds, he could not bear the light, and he did not open his eyes and kept thinking about Thanatos. A couple of minutes passed and he fainted.

Percy, Vulcan, and Alessandra were riding but Percy was very curious and asked, "Will you bother to tell me where are we going?" Vulcan chuckled and said, "If I tell you, you might get scared and run off." Percy felt those words like a hundred arrows had gone through him simultaneously. He replied in anger, "Don't you dare say that, there is not a thing in this whole world that can scare me off." Alessandra was secretly laughing as she didn't want Percy to see it. "I do not care how frightening it is, I need to know where we are headed." Vulcan was unsure but still wanted Percy to know about it, "We are going to Sousaki." Alessandra's facial expressions changed immediately, she said in a terrified voice, "You can't take us there, it's a death wish." Percy didn't know what they were talking about, "But why, Alessandra?" Alessandra said once again, "You don't know, it's a volcano. It is far more dangerous than anything you've come across." Vulcan smiled and said, "Oh dear, you don't know everything, do you? I thought being the princess of Delphi you would know more than that. Sousaki being a volcano isn't the danger I was talking about." Alessandra was really confused now, but Percy was even more lost than her, "I don't know what you are talking about, but as I said, I do not care where or what it is I will become stronger than anyone in this world." Vulcan nodded and said, "Then so be it."

Solaris along with Nathan, Atreus, and Aetios who was still unconscious was going to the dwelling of the Oracle. Atreus was very curious to know about the summons and wanted to know what his summon was, "I wanted to know more about summoning, please tell me." Solaris was focused on the situation at hand but still said, "I cannot teach you everything now but I will give you the most important advice, you have to understand that the summon is like a gift from your soul, if your thoughts are not clear you cannot summon." Nathan was listening closely but didn't feel like he was going to need it. They had arrived at the house but Nathan noticed something straight away, there were no guards outside the house, it was strange as the Oracle was a well-respected figure in every city. They entered one by one but saw no one, the house courtyard was open at the top and had rooms on all four sides. Solaris was about to speak, "I am Sol…" when a thin female voice interrupted him, "Solaris, the Golden Knight, you are here to seek the Gates Of Hades." Atreus said, "Not this again, how does she know what we are going to say." She spoke again when a very slim woman dressed in all-white robes came out through the curtains, "It is because you all walk on the path destined for you by the Gods." Nathan was still not quite sure how she walked through the curtains when the other side had a wall. Solaris did not want to waste any time, "So can you please lead us towards the Gates Of Hades?" She smiled and said elegantly, "Oh sure, I was just waiting for the Heir of Leonidas to wake up, he might have something important to tell us." As she said this, they all saw Aetios' face sweating and he was giving strange gestures. Nathan was worried, "What is happening?" Aetios jumped up in fear and looked around in awe, he could not comprehend what was happening but what he saw in his vision was far more important than knowing where he was. The oracle spoke again, "Oh! you woke up sooner than I thought you would, now can you please share with your friends what you saw." Aetios was still shocked and said, "I... I saw Sparta, burning and Deimos was there, it felt so real. We were all there, fighting him, but we were losing, we didn't have enough strength." Atreus and Nathan were worried, Solaris said, "We need to inform someone in Sparta about the attack." Aetios said, "Yes, we have to send a message to Theseus." The oracle chuckled and replied, "I think he already knows" as she pointed her finger towards Ikaros who was soaring in the skies above them. She continued, "Theseus can delay the army of Deimos but you all need to get the Blades of Hades as quickly as possible." Atreus spoke in a sarcastic voice, "Yes, but it would be much easier if you just told us where the Gates of Hades were." "The path to Hades starts at the rock bottom of the Greek island in Taenarum. Now off you go." Aetios had one last question before leaving, "But what if we cannot defeat Deimos?" The oracle said, "The results of most wars in the human race are already destined but generational kids like yourselves who have powers of the Gods can do anything if you believe in yourselves. Just remember to never give up." Atreus said, "I have heard that one a few times."

Chapter 9

THE GOD OF DEATH

Eivor didn't know what was happening but still had his eyes closed. He heard Angelos say, "You did it, open your eyes now." As Eivor opened his eyes he saw a completely dark road with a purple sky and black clouds. It was like everything was much darker yet he could see everything including Angelos. Eivor asked, "How can I see you when there is no light?" Angelos was quite serious and said, "Save your questions for Thanatos." Angelos helped him up and they both walked towards a large gate that had an engraving saying "Death Awaits." Both of them entered the rather unpleasant city, Angelos had been there but Eivor was a little startled by a familiar feeling. Angelos said, "Believe me it's not as bad as you think, it is a ghost city. All the souls who cannot pass the river Styx come here and roam for eternity. Eivor laughed and said, "None of the other guys would have survived this sight, Percy might have the strongest odds of surviving here." They both walked through the vacant streets, with strange noises coming from all directions. Eivor was tired of not knowing things, "Where do we find Thanatos?" "He is usually in his castle, that's the only place I have seen him in." Eivor was curious, he didn't fit in the real world, he always felt separated and did not feel the nature there. Now he could feel the energy, he felt more powerful than he had ever felt before. They reached the huge gates of the castle, it was like a never-ending wall which seemed like touching the Moon. Eivor said, "So, how are we able to get in then?" Angelos smiled, and said, "You don't know anything about your powers, do you?" Eivor was frustrated that a kid was insulting him, "Tell me then," Angelos just walked right through the wall. Eivor was startled and was unsure about following him but he still walked through it "How can we walk through it?" Angelos was tired of answering questions, he sighed and said, "You need to know more about your powers to understand these things. You are the master of the underworld. Do you think the only power you have is to talk to souls?" Eivor thought about that, "But how am I going to learn more about my powers." "You need to think like Hades and Thanatos might be able to help you." They walked into the even darker throne room, they tried to look for The God of Death but couldn't see anything. Angelos shouted, "We need help, Lord Thanatos." An eerie feeling got hold of Eivor and

Angelos and a really low but deep voice said, "What is it that you seek?" Eivor somehow managed to speak, "We need to go to the underworld and come back." Suddenly the whole room lit up and they saw a huge man with purple and black robes sitting on the throne. "That's a bold ask young man, might I ask the reason for going there?" They were startled by the sight of Thanatos. Eivor said, "I need to get the Blades Of Hades." "That's a lie, no one can see them other than Hades himself, even if you go there you won't be able to get them." Angelos had to step in, "He's back, Lord Deimos." The look on Thanatos's face changed from anger to concern, "It can't be. That means the Olympians have been assembled." Angelos did not want to say it but he could not hide anything from him, "Not quite yet, the reincarnations of Athena, Dionysus, Demeter, and Aphrodite are still unknown." "By the sight of it, this one also still doesn't realize how great his powers are, Angelos go and grab the ring of Purgatory from my vault. I will have a word with our friend here." Angelos went away, Thanatos stood up from his throne, he was almost as big as the pillar behind him. Eivor was in awe, he came up to him, raised his hand, and summoned a black helmet. Eivor said, "What is that?" "This is the Helm of Darkness." Eivor remembered Vulcan telling him about it. Thanatos continued, "This was entrusted to me by Hades himself for one day to give it to a warrior like you. This can make you go invisible, well not really.

You can go into the dark dimension that is a parallel universe to this one but no one else can see you." He handed it over to him and Eivor held it in front and was admiring it when he saw Angelos coming back, so he immediately put it on his head. Angelos came in with the ring of Purgatory and said, "Where is he gone?" Thanatos didn't say a word. Eivor touched the top of his head but Angelos was clueless, "No, tell me where is he? What have you told him?" Thanatos said, "Come back now, I did not finish." Eivor took the helmet off and was visible again. Angelos was a bit confused but didn't ask any questions. Thanatos continued, "This is just one part of your powers, you need to get the Blades to unlock your true potential, you are the commander of every soul in this entire world, remember that. Once you have the Blades of Hades, you will be able to summon any soul at will but use it very carefully because it can backfire if you use it too often. Show this ring to Chairon, the Ferryman and he will grant you passage to the underworld but be careful, not everyone is welcome in the kingdom of Hades."

Percy, Alessandra, and Vulcan had reached the foothills of Sousaki, Vulcan said, "This is our first stop. We will be starting your practice here." Percy started getting ready for the practice, Alessandra asked Vulcan, "Why are we doing this now? Aetios and the others need him." Vulcan replied gently, "They can hold their own in the underworld but if and when Deimos returns, it will be difficult for them to deal with him. Atreus and Nathan have not yet unlocked their potential. Eivor has still not got the hang of his powers and even with the Blades of Hades, he will not be able to master them in a short time. Aetios is the only one who can go toe to toe with Deimos. If Percy masters the way of Ares he can be a catalyst for the destruction of Deimos, Moreover, he needs to hone his anger to use the Sword of Ares." Alessandra was surprised, "The sword of Ares? How do you know about this?" Vulcan chuckled and replied, "Things are not necessarily what they seem, young lady. I have lived for a millennium now, I have seen kings rise and die. I have seen cities burnt to the ground and new ones born from those ashes. I trained a young Spartan, he was fierce too and stubborn." Alessandra's eyes expanded and she was shaking, "What was his name?" Vulcan sighed and said, "The greatest king Sparta has seen, Leonidas. Do not speak about any of this to Percy. You see, people waste their lives searching for power but they do not realize that the greatest person a human can have is his mind. I will tell them myself when the time is right, but for now, let's train our God of War."

In a throne room of a castle that nobody knew the location of, Deimos was starting to worry about Aetios as he was learning about his powers which he could feel it. He wanted to know what the future holds, he wanted to know about Aetios and the others. Deimos along with Dunamis, a tall and muscular man who was wearing a purple cape with silver armour, wanted to meet the oracle of Delphi. Deimos summoned a huge black pegasus to fly there, Dunamis did not need a summon to fly he could control clouds and could fly on them. It was a very strange sight but many other unimaginable things were yet to happen. Both of them flew to the top of a mountain near the castle, there was a triangular gateway made out of obsidian, both of them went through it and reached Delphi in no time. Unlike normal people, they just smashed through the temple and saw that she was not there. The gatekeeper informed them that she was at her house so they rushed there in a hurry. They arrived minutes after Solaris and the others had left the place, Dunamis kicked the doors in and both of them entered the house at the same time. Deimos said, "Tell me, lady, what does my future hold?" The oracle was very calm and collected, "Why are you rushing things so much? You have just entered my house, would you like to drink anything?" Deimos was angry, "Don't you try to play mind games with me, just tell me what I want to know." The oracle stood up, looked up towards the sky, and said, "That's your demise up there." Deimos quickly looked up and tried to see what it was but he could not see anything but clouds. The oracle said, "Look closely." Deimos saw a cloud in the shape of a dragon which widened his eyes. He was even more furious, he said, "Dunamis kill her so that nobody else can know about it." Dunamis walked heavily toward the oracle, she took a few steps backwards and said, "It's a curious thing isn't it, people come to me to know more about their future but they don't consider the possibility of my destiny." She whistled, a Pheonix flew and a fire burst blinding the eyes of the duo for a moment. As Deimos opened his eyes the oracle was gone, he cried, "No!! Dunamis we need to ensure that nobody else knows about this. Dunamis nodded but now Deimos was very concerned about the prophecy told by the oracle.

Chapter 10

A TUSSLE AT TAENARUM

Aetios, Solaris, Atreus, and Nathan had almost reached Taenarum. Aetios signaled Ikaros to go and find Eivor and Angelos, he did not have a good feeling about this place. Atreus asked Solaris, "When are you going to teach me about summoning?" Solaris chuckled and said, "I have said it before and I will say it again, summoning is not that can be taught just like that. It has to come from your heart. You need to understand yourself before you can start summoning, you must align your thoughts with the desire of your heart then only you can summon something." Aetios was listening closely to this conversation, he was also curious about summoning and asked, "But what can one summon?" Solaris' face lit up in joy and said, "I love it, you being so curious. I can only imagine the level of power you will have once you realize your potential, anyways there are two different summons.

There is a spirit summon and a weapon summon. The spirit summon might be a war summon or a locomotive summon. The weapon summon on the other hand can only be done with weapons such as the Spear of Leonidas." Aetios, Atreus, and Nathan were all in awe after hearing this. As they were talking about this, they reached Taenarum. It was a foggy, quiet, and eerie place, it sure looked like the entrance to the underworld. Atreus said, "How are we going to find the Gates of Hades in this mess?" Nathan stood and said, "Just get me down there, I can do this." Nathan was feeling very useless for some time, he thought he could be really helpful in a place like this." Atreus and Solaris were reluctant about his idea but Aetios trusted him, "Solaris will get the chariot down and you can do whatever you want." Nathan was grateful for Aetios's trust, he knew he had to grab this chance. They jumped out of the chariot as it disappeared into Solaris's hand, Solaris said, "Show us what you got, Nathan." He quickly knelt and put his left hand on the ground. Everyone else was confused but Nathan could feel the whole place, it was like he could see through his senses. Nathan said, "I am feeling an energy, it's quite far away but it's a lot." He tried to get closer to that energy but could not place it. He warned Aetios, "Someone is coming our way and it's not Eivor or Angelos." Aetios was quickly alerted and said, "Solaris, Atreus form a triangle around Nathan and watch out for any attack that comes your way.

Nathan keep looking for the gates, we will protect you." Solaris was looking closely in the fog and saw a mace coming his way, he quickly deflected it and said, "Oh! I get it now it's Dunamis, one of Deimos's generals. That explains the fog everywhere, he is fighting to his advantage." As he was saying that Atreus suddenly fell to the ground, and they had to come up with a plan. Aetios said, "Solaris, just look after Atreus, me and Nathan will finish the job here." Solaris quickly picked up Atreus and started flying up in the chariot, Aetios struck the spear in the ground and it happened once again, golden red armor started appearing on him and a helmet with a wolf on top of it appeared in his hand. Aetios said, "Just focus on Dunamis now and tell me from which direction is the attack coming." Nathan agreed and they were ready, Aetios also closed his eyes to channel his focus. Nathan shouted, "LEFT". He quickly deflected it and said, "Just one more time, I've got him." Nathan patiently waited for the next attack and shouted again, "LEFT", this time Aetios pinned the chain of that mace down on the ground and started pulling it towards him. Dunamis could not pull the mace back as the Spear of Leonidas did not obey anybody other than Aetios, but he was struggling to pull Dunamis towards him. Aetios shouts, "Solaris form a light dome around me and Dunamis, I will fight him. You take care of Nathan and Atreus." Solaris was a bit doubtful about his strategy but he still trusted him and did it. There was no fog inside the dome, Dunamis saw him and said, "Do you have a death wish kid, trying to fight me?" Aetios smirked and said, "We will see about that." They both ran towards each other with Aetios holding the spear and Dunamis with his mace. The latter swung it while running but Aetios jumped over it and shoved him in the face with the back end of the spear, Dunamis pulled his mace back which hit him from behind. It made him fall to the ground, the big guy went for another strike to end it all but Aetios was quick enough to roll out of the way. He tapped the spear on the ground and entered the wolf mode, being much quicker, now he attacked Dunamis with a series of blows that left him vulnerable. The eagle visioned saw an opening near his belly, he went for a strike but to his horror Dunamis caught him by the neck and slammed him hard onto the ground. Aetios was hurt and could barely move but managed to get up. Suddenly, he saw that Danumis had stopped moving, everything went black and now he was in Sparta where he saw Leonidas defending his hometown against an army of soldiers, their king sat on an elephant at the farthest side of the battlefield, the Spartans were fighting very bravely but the enemy king could not be reached at that height. Even the archers could not reach from this distance. Leonidas had to do something, he threw his spear with full power towards the king's head but he moved out of the way and it got stuck in his throne. While he was laughing to see Leonidas miss, he vanished from the battlefield and appeared on the elephant behind the enemy king, he pulled the spear out and pierced it through his head. Everyone was shocked and started running away. Aetios thought how can someone just teleport like that? As he was thinking he came back to the present and saw Dunamis coming towards him, swinging the mace to deal the final blow. Aetios looked carefully but was not able to find anything, but he had an idea. The biggest gamble he had ever taken, he threw his spear at Dunamis which he dodged but that's what he wanted. The spear landed behind him, Aetios closed his eyes and tried to replicate Leonidas but nothing worked, Dunamis was coming closer and closer. Aetios whispered, "How did you do that? Leonidas, help me!" As the mace was about to smash through him, a bright golden light engulfed Aetios and he vanished on the spot. Dunamis was clueless, he swayed his head from side to side but could not see Aetios, "Look here, you knave." Aetios was standing right behind him and struck his spear but Dunamis moved and it hit his arm instead. He immediately tried to run off but had nowhere to go. He screamed, "Deimos, bring me back now." Aetios called back his spear as he started running towards him but a black portal opened behind Dunamis. He said, "I will be back, kid" as he entered the portal. Aetios almost had him but was disappointed, the light dome vanished as the duel was over. The fog was gone, Nathan had done it, and Aetios could see the Gates of Hades in the distance. It was an eerie sight to see, the gates were black and gold with three dog heads sculpted in the middle. Solaris, Nathan, and Atreus were already there, as Aetios was running towards them he heard Ikaros's screech, he wasn't sure if it had found Eivor and Angelos. Aetios reached the trio and said, "Ikaros is back, maybe Eivor and Angelos are on their way." As he was talking, somebody slapped him on his head. He turned around but no one was there, it happened again, he felt a slap on his head but no one was behind. He said, "What is happening?" Atreus and Nathan were laughing continuously. Finally, Eivor appeared in front of them out of nowhere. Everyone was confused, Angelos ran in and stood next to him. Solaris said, "Eivor and Atreus, its good to see you again. Would you mind sharing your experience with the God Of Death with us." Eivor was very excited to tell everyone about the Helm of Darkness." Angelos said, "The good news is we can now enter the underworld without worrying about the external threat but the internal trials remain to be unfolded." Atreus was a bit startled, "What do you mean by that?" Solaris intervened, "You see, the underworld is not a place fit for humans. The weather conditions are extreme to start with but that's just the tip of the iceberg, the five rivers of the underworld are a challenge even for the most skilled warrior. If you somehow went past them, the three parts of Hades await you with not just physical but mental tests as well. One must only enter The Gates of Hades if they have the guts." Everyone was serious now, they knew it was going to be a hard journey ahead and they would have to work together in order to make it out alive. Aetios said, "Just know I will give my life to defend my comrades in battle and I hope everyone thinks the same way. This is the spartan way."

Chapter 11

WELCOME TO HADES

Aetios stepped up to the gate and tried to push it but it wouldn't open. Everyone was trying something, Eivor had an idea, he put on the Helm of Darkness and tried to push through the door, he immediately went through. He could not believe his eyes, it was the darkest place he had ever seen, he was on the edge of a river which was a bit strange on its own. The river was yellow, he had never seen something like this. Eivor was confused now, how could he let everybody else in? As he was thinking about it he heard creepy noises, they kept getting louder every second. On the other side of the gates, Solaris had a plan ready. He had figured out the secret of the door, it was a puzzle. There were three sigils on the door, the first one was three trees with a person sitting underneath the middle one. The second one was a palace with rays of light coming out from it. The third sigil was also a palace but this one had no light rays, it was on the back of a giant. Atreus said, "What are we meant to do with these?" Solaris was not sure but Angelos had something to say, "They are the three parts of the underworld." He started rearranging them and putting them in a vertical line. As the sigils came into place the gates opened, everyone was a bit confused about the sigils but they believed each other. Solaris and Aetios entered the realm of Hades first but could not see Eivor anywhere, Atreus and Angelos followed them and Nathan entered at last. They could see a cave up ahead but could not even see a single soul, literally. Solaris asked Angelos, "What can you tell me about this cave?" He replied in a rather low voice, "I am afraid I can't tell you what this cave holds but I can tell you its name, Hypnos." Aetios was quick to answer, "I think we need to go in anyway. Just stay on your toes." The team walked into the dark cave not knowing what awaited them.

Dunamis had returned to Deimos, he was tired, broken, and defeated, something he had never experienced before. Deimos was furious, he levitated him into the air and said, "Give me one good reason to spare your life." Dunamis was screaming as Pyrrhus and Kari watched him fearfully. There were two other people in the hall as well, both were smiling at his suffering. Dunamis said, "I had him right in front of me but he used his spear to teleport." Deimos's expression changed instantly, "Oh, he is learning fast, this is not a time for punishments. Gather our army, sharpen your blades, we are going to war soon. Until then, I have a quest of my own." He opened a portal and disappeared instantly. Everyone else in the hall quickly started preparing for the war.

Aetios was leading the pack into cave Hypnos, they could barely traverse through the uneven terrain. Angelos was pretty impatient, "I will go and scout ahead." Nathan could sense something ahead and said, "Aetios I can sense a really strong aura ahead, we should wait for Angelos to return." Aetios was adamant on finding Eivor, "We need to move quickly, there is no time to sit around and wait." They all reached an opening where they could see Angelos waving to them. They all reached a river where a ferryman was standing with a boat, they could see floating mountains in the distance with no way to get to them. Aetios exclaimed, "Look! What are those." Angelos said, "It's the Elysium." Everyone was silent for a second, it was a sight to behold. It would be an understatement to call it beautiful. Angelos said, "We need to give Chairon the ring of Thanatos." He was wearing a dark green robe and had a stick in his hand, "Let's go then" Solaris replied. All of them sat on the boat and the boat started moving towards the central island, Nathan thought of talking to Chairon but resisted the urge as he looked creepy. As soon as they set foot on it, a sword came flying in and landed right at Aetios's foot, "Who is that?" A rather sweet and melodious voice said, "You shouldn't be here." Aetios replied, "I would say we are more deserving of being here than someone who doesn't even show her face." A girl appeared from out of nowhere, she had deep blue eyes, black hair, and leather armor. Aetios was speechless at first, it was like he had seen an angel. She said, "Tell me the purpose of your visit or I would have to force you out of here." Angelos said, "I think I should do the talking part, Aetios is somewhat new to these lands." She said in a firm voice, "No, I want him to speak to me, after all, he has the Spear of Leonidas." Aetios quickly drew out the spear, put it on her neck, and said, "I will talk, we are here to get the Blades of Hades, our friend Eivor is also missing," She said, "Oh that cocky one is your friend?" Aetios said, "Yes and you will take me to him, or else this spear will go through your neck in an instant." She took them to him. All of them ran towards the palace, Eivor was sitting on the table and eating food. Aetios said, "Are you alright Eivor?" He could barely speak, "Yes I am more than fine, they are treating me nice." Everybody else was hungry as well, they all started devouring the food. Aetios still had his suspicions and asked the girl, "What is your name?" She smiled and said, "Zinovia." Aetios smiled back and said, "What do you do here Zinovia?" She said, "I live here in the Elysium, I died many years ago, according to your time I am probably more than 100 years old." Aetios was not surprised at all, he had already judged that after seeing her courage when standing at the end of a spear blade. Only a true warrior would have such conviction in one's eyes at such a time. Aetios did not usually trust people but he believed Zinovia. He continued, "Do you know where we can find the Blades Of Hades?" Zinovia said, "They can only be found in the depths of Tarturus by the king of the underworld." Aetios giggled and said, "Well at least we have the king here, we just need to get to Tarturus now." "It's easier said than done, the place is filled with the most evil people from the past generations." As they were talking, Aetios noticed Ikaros screeching, he closed his eyes and heard Theseus, "Aetios you need to find the Blades quickly, I have got news of a possible attack on Sparta by Deimos." He quickly opened his eyes and said, "We need to go now." Zinovia calmed him down and said, "Wait! what happened?" "Deimos is going to attack Sparta, we need to get there." Aetios rushed to the table and said, "Everyone, listen to me. Sparta is in danger but we need to get the Blades first. We will split into three teams, , Eivor and Zinovia will go into Tarturus to retrieve the Blades. Solaris, Atreus, and Nathan will go to Sparta and help Theseus, as for Angelos, he and Ikaros will go and get reinforcements. Solaris quickly departed with Nathan and Atreus.

Theseus was in the Spartan castle preparing for the attack, and a Spartan soldier asked, “But, sir how do we know for certain that Deimos is coming to attack us?” Theseus stared right into his eyes and said, “I have lived long enough to know some valuable people who bring with them valuable information. Even if one of his generals steps foot in here we would get to know. Go to the northern gates, some ‘heroes’ will be arriving soon. Bring them to me.”

Chapter 12

THE QUEST AGAINST TIME

Solaris, Atreus, and Nathan were flying towards Sparta on the Chariot. Nathan asked, "Are we going to war?" Solaris said, "We cannot take any chances, Aetios believes Theseus, so I do. We have to reach Sparta as soon as possible." Nathan was anxious, he had never fought a battle before. Atreus said, "Nathan, we need to fight with our life on the line we cannot let Deimos get any of the weapons." They reached the gates of Sparta in a few hours, two guards were standing there waiting for them, Solaris just ignored them and flew right past. They flew straight towards the royal palace. It was like a small city in Sparta itself, filled with Spartan soldiers. The palace itself was an eternal beauty, but the garden right in front of the gates was something one could only dream about, it was a shame they had to land the chariot on that perfect grass, it was like someone had cut every single plant separately. They got out of the chariot and went straight to Theseus. Theseus was talking to Solanke, one of Sparta's generals. Solaris said, "I had only heard stories about you, a man who could crush entire armies under the sole of his boot, a man who could cut down any creature in the whole world with just one swing of his sword. Have you got one more war in you?" Theseus turned around and said, "It's not my duty to save the world, but it is my responsibility to save Sparta. I will never let anything happen to this city. If Deimos wants to destroy Sparta, he will have to go through every single one of these soldiers here." The tension in that room was till the roof, Nathan and Atreus were speechless, Solaris moved his hand towards Theseus for a handshake and said, "Let's do this." Theseus grabbed his hand firmly and said, "For Sparta."

On a different side of Greece, Percy was training to control his powers. Vulcan had started his tasks, "Boy, you need to do three simple things to convince me that you are ready for the power of Ares, until then you are cuffed." Vulcan swung his arm vigorously from side to side and a glowing white thread started floating around Percy and then disappeared. Alessandra was worried, "What have you done?" "Percy needs to control his anger to realize his power but whenever he is out of control his powers take control of him. He needs to take over his mind. For the first task, you have to sit on a wooden slab near the tip of the volcano, but I will be heating the volcano." Percy said, "What are you waiting for then?" Percy sat down on the wooden slab in the center of the volcano which now had no hole in it because it had been dormant for centuries. Vulcan slammed his foot on the ground and the top of the volcano crumbled leaving only Percy in the middle of it. They could see the lava inside the volcano. This time, Vulcan raised his arm and the lava rose gradually surrounding Percy in lava. Vulcan said, "The first test will be that you have to break that seal put on you but it will not be broken with anger but with acceptance. You need to accept the facts that haunt you and until then nobody will talk to you." Vulcan went away and took Alessandra with him. Percy couldn't understand what he had to do to complete this task, he sat down and closed his eyes. Percy was an ice man, he appeared to be hard from the outside but could melt in an instant. Alessandra asked Vulcan, "What is this all about?" Vulcan smiled and said, "My dear, you met the Percy who had healed himself from his wounds but as they say, wounds heal, scars don't." Alessandra was startled by Vulcan and said, "What was he like before? Before the wounds." Vulcan replied, "Let me tell you a story, I was in Sparta many years ago serving as Leonidas's advisor. After he died, I served Sparta with my life but when the Battle of Plataea ended, I could not bear the loss of so many of my comrades. So, I entrusted Theseus with the task of protecting Sparta and the prophecy left behind by

Leonidas. Percy's father was there too, Amompharetus, the man with irreproachable valor. He fought valiantly but could not survive the war. Percy was shaken by the news of his father's death, shortly after this his mother passed away due to an illness. He had barely moved on from that when he had to join training for the army. He could not let go of his parents's passing away. He has no other fear in his heart but he needs to let go of this. When he met you he was held up by his friend, Aetios. He sees him as the most prized possession of his life." Alessandra was speechless, she did not know about any of this. She always thought of Percy as a brave warrior but a cold person. Vulcan further added, "He thinks that he can save everyone alone but he needs to realize the importance of teamwork."

Aetios, Zinovia, and Eivor were also on the move. They were standing at the entrance to Tarturus. Aetios said, "Before going in, Zinovia, can you tell us what to expect in there?" Zinovia replied with gaping eyes, "I haven't been there myself but I have heard stories that many creatures roam Tarturus that are not friendly and can even attack on site. We can expect a warm welcome from them as well as the lava pouring down from everywhere." Aetios shook his head and said, "I have a plan, Eivor is the only one able to get the blades of Hades, Zinovia and I will hold any creatures from getting to Eivor. He will have enough time to get in there and get out easily, once we have the blades, we need to make a run back here. Is it clear?" Both Zinovia and Eivor nodded in agreement. Eivor touched the entrance and it opened up slowly. They could see creatures flying everywhere and the heat of the place was even coming through to them. Aetios looked at Eivor and nodded, he turned his head to Zinovia and nodded again saying, "Let's do this." They ran into Tarturus, onto a bridge and at the end of it was a huge black gate. Aetios pointed towards the gate and said, "Eivor run." Aetios pointed to the sky and said, "Zinovia, shoot as many of those creatures as you can." She pulled out her bow and arrow and started shooting the creatures in the sky. Aetios ran with Eivor to escort him to the gate. Many dog-like creatures started appearing from under the bridge. They looked familiar to Aetios and Eivor. Eivor said, "They are Deimos' army, but how are they here?" Aetios said, "We can worry about that later, now let's finish what we have started." Aetios threw his spear at the dogs which pierced through two of them, he then held Eivor's hand and teleported him behind the dogs with himself and said, "Go now, I will take care of this."

Chapter 13

THE TASK AT HAND

Percy was still sitting in the middle of the volcano pondering about the words of Vulcan. He always had something in his mind, he always knew the solution to the problem but this time he was clueless. Until now he could just cut through his problems with his sword but now it was not the case anymore. He started talking to himself, "I need to think, I should be able to get out of this, I am never clueless." He thought thoroughly and got lost in his memories, "I have killed a lot of people but until now I couldn't comprehend the amount of people I killed. Maybe it is something within me that urges me to kill. It has been far too long, I need to be a better man, for me, for Alessandra, for my parents." As he was saying this he opened his eyes and saw himself sitting under an Oak tree, he could not help but notice a house with a horse hitched outside. Percy got up and started walking towards the house. He recognized the hut as his old house outside Sparta. As he got closer he heard voices coming from the house, "Percy stop, you will tire yourself out. *Pater* will be here soon, go and wash your hands for dinner." Percy instantly remembered that day, hardly had he worked his brain before two spartan guards came galloping at the front gate. It was like Percy wasn't even there, nobody could see him. Percy's mother, Sofia ran out thinking that it would be Amompharetus, but the soldiers said, "We are here to inform you that Amompharetus has been killed and will receive a proper burial tomorrow in the castle. Sofia broke down into tears on the pavement of the door. She could not breathe properly, little Percy walked up to the door and said, "Mater, what happened, why are you crying?" Sofia could barely speak and said, "Nothing… nothing happened, they said that Pater won't come home today." Percy asked again, "So, when will he be back?" Sofia could not hold her tears and hugged the little boy. Percy was confused and was out of words, poor Sofia had nothing to say to the boy. Upon seeing all of this, Percy had a tear in his eye but wiped it straight away. He started running back to the oak tree, but every step he took just took him away from that tree. He could not move from his place. He closed his eyes again and thought to himself the words of Vulcan, "He told me to let go, I could not quite understand what he was saying but now I know what all he was talking about, I need to let go of my past. It is controlling my powers, I need to get hold of my consciousness. He opened his eyes and instead of running away from the incident, he walked up to it and hugged his mother. As soon as he did that the horse hitched outside and started rearing, Percy walked up to it and patted it. Slowly, everything except the oak tree and the horse disappeared. Percy got on the horse and started riding towards the Oak tree, as he got closer, the tree trunk tore apart and created a passage for him to go through. He leaped into the passage and ended up where he started, in the middle of the volcano surrounded by lava. As he stood up, threads of light started flying from his belly and disappeared into the sky. Vulcan said, "Well done, boy." Percy was caught off guard by him and said, "What now?" Alessandra was standing behind Vulcan and looked worried. Vulcan said, "Follow me" and jumped right into the lava. Percy was a bit hesitant, he could not get himself to jump into the pit of lava. Alessandra also started shouting, "Percy don't do it, I cannot let you die." Percy had to make a choice, either follow Vulcan into the lava or listen to Alessandra. Percy said, "Alessandra I know you worry about me constantly but the truth is to save the world. I need to master my powers. I need to help Aetios. He instantly jumped into the pool of lava. He could not see anything and just kept falling endlessly. He was about to hit the ground but Vulcan instantly caught him on a mattress made out of air. It was nothing like a volcano but was much larger and spacious than he could imagine. Percy said, "You have used that magic after a long time." Vulcan grinned and said, "Don't worry about it, you have passed two tests out of three. I instructed Alessandra to try and stop you from jumping in here. You showed strength and guts in coherence with emotional stability. I think you are ready for the final task." Percy smiled and said, "I am ready for anything old man, even you." Vulcan said mockingly, "I'm sure you are. Now let's take a look into what your task is. You have to enter the doorway there and come out alive." Percy said, "Sounds easy enough" and started walking towards the door, little did he know he was about to face one of the biggest challenges of his life.

For Aetios and Zinovia, things weren't going so well. They were standing outside the entrance to the Blades of Hades. Aetios said as he swung his spear and cut off the head of a creature, "Just follow my lead and we will make it out of here alive." Zinovia fired an arrow into the neck of another one and said, "I can do just well on my own, you know." A dog was about to lunge on Zinovia but Aetios threw his spear to pin it to the ground and said, "I know what I am doing." He held her arm to pull Zinovia towards him and said, "Look into my eyes Zinovia, do I look like a person who would let anyone touch my comrades? I am from Sparta, our lifestyle is fighting and leading armies. We go into a battle knowing that there will be only two outcomes, either we win the battle or we die trying." He called his spear back and split another creature in half, "I just want to win this battle against Deimos with the least number of casualties." Zinovia was shaken by his words and said, "Let's do this your way then." Aetios said, "Stand here with your bow and focus on the enemies coming from above, I will deal with the ones on the bridge." He threw his spear into another Azazel and then teleported into a group of four. He jumped up and tapped the tip of his spear to enter wolf mode. Zinovia stood in awe to see Aetios just slit through every Azazel standing there in an instant, he shouted, "Zinovia, hold your ground." She got out of the shock and started raining arrows.

Eivor went inside and saw a throne room, there were large webs surrounding the whole room. He walked further and saw a corpse sitting on the throne. He looked closely and saw a green glimmer near its hand, he slowly walked towards it but heard some disturbances at the other end of the room but still carried on. He could see the corpse was holding the blades. He grabbed the blades out of the corpse's hand, but as soon as he did that something jumped out from behind the throne and landed behind Eivor. Eivor turned around and saw six red eyes glowing. He took a step back but the eyes got bigger and that thing got even closer. As the light hit the creature, Eivor could see a dog but it was a lot bigger than normal dogs, Eivor was shocked when he saw that the dog had three heads. Eivor looked at the gem in his silver blade which had a purple handle, upon closer inspection Eivor saw that it had the words "Persephone" engraved on one blade and "Hades" on the other. The dog barked and Eivor could see fire in his mouth. The green gem glowed and a soul flew out of the corpse. Eivor said, "Who are you?" The soul answered, "It doesn't matter who I am, what matters is that you learn the powers of those blades in your hands. The soul flew towards the angry dog and calmed it down. Eivor said, "So, you are Hades." Hades replied laughingly, "Well, you are not as dumb as I thought you would be." Eivor was a bit ashamed but didn't want to show it. Hades continued, "I am very happy that I am free from the duty of holding those blades, but I was instructed to tell their successor what to do with them. I would have just given them to you but orders are orders." Eivor was not expecting such loose talk from the God of the Underworld. Hades got closer to him and said, "These blades give you quite a lot of privileges, some of which you might have already experienced. You can talk to any soul in the underworld, Tarturus is off-limits. The blades can help you bring any person to life granted that they are willing to come back. Lastly, you can split your soul into different bodies to make clones of yourself, although making a large number of clones will take you practice." He got close to his ear and said, "That's how I met all the ladies at once. The powers of those blades are endless and are dependent on the user's capability." He took a long breath and said, "I have remembered those lines for so long. It is like some heavy burden got off my shoulders." He shook Eivor's hand and said, "I don't care what is happening in the upperworld but I wish you the best of luck for your adventures ahead." He flew right back into the corpse and Cerberus went to sleep again. Eivor was out of words on what had just happened. He thought of calling Hades back to ask him some questions but he popped out of the corpse and said, "I will not be answering your callout, Thank you." He disappeared right back into the corpse.

Aetios and Zinovia had got rid of most of the Azazel, Aetios said, "We got most of them." Zinovia smiled back at him and said, "Wouldn't expect anything less from the heir of Zeus." Aetios felt something he had not felt for a long time, he felt the presence of love in her smile, but they could not finish their conversation as the bridge suddenly started shaking. Zinovia said, "What now?" Aetios grabbed her arm with one hand and pulled her behind him. They saw a manticore appear from the bridge. Aetios said, "Attack on my call, I have killed it before, I can do it again." Aetios knew that it would shoot stings from its scorpion tail and could use its fangs as well. He was ready for anything the Manticore had to offer. The Manticore started running towards the duo, Aetios stood his ground for a moment and then whispered, "On my call, you go right and I will jump left." As the beast came closer Aetios shouted, "NOW" and both of them jumped the opposite way. The Manticore stood there confused, he moved right and his tail rose, he was about to shoot a sting at Zinovia but Aetios appeared from under the Manticore and swung the spear across his face. The vexed creature growled and stepped back. Zinovia said, "How did you do that?" Aetios said, "When we jumped, I left the spear on the ground and then just teleported to it." Aetios again put his spear up and was ready for the fight, before he could make a move a blade came flying in from behind them and hit the Manticore right in the eye. Both Aetios and Zinovia were startled, the blade flew right back from where it came from. Aetios looked back and saw Eivor walking towards them while tossing the blades from one hand to the other. Aetios had a smile on his face, "I knew he would do it." Eivor said, "I met Hades and I got to know so much. It was truly something out of an epic." Aetios said, "We have to go to Sparta now, Deimos needs to be stopped and it will happen today." Zinovia had her head hung down and said, "So, I think this is where we part ways then." Aetios felt his heart sink for the first time in his life, "There must be some way we could take you with us." Zinovia nodded her head and said, "No power other than the king of Hades can grant this permission." Eivor fake coughed and started smiling. Aetios and Zinovia looked at him for a split second and instantly hugged him. Aetios said, "Let's do this the Spartan way."

Chapter 14

THE DRAGON REBORN

Percy entered the door into an arena, it was quite dark, and he could not see anything. Percy said, "So I just have to stand here." Hardly had he said that, he heard a growl behind him but he could see nothing in such darkness. Percy pulled Hofund out of its sheath and slowly started walking towards the sound, he shouted, "Come on, show yourself." Instantly he saw a huge stream of fire coming his way, it was so quick that he could barely dodge it. Percy was clueless, barely had he picked himself up, when felt the gust of wings. He knew that vision was needed if he wanted to fight this creature. He tried to remember Vulcan's words, but he could barely recall anything. Suddenly, he heard a deep loud voice, "Percy, listen to me. Use the will of fire." Percy could not see anyone but he knew that whoever it was, it was trying to help him. He looked at his hand and attempted to channel his power, unlike the other times, it came naturally to him this time. A small flame ignited in his hand, he smiled and waved his hand in the air to create a ring of fire, it lit up the room and Percy could see the creature properly now. He looked closely and saw red feathers, he tried to attack it but it rose in the air and started circling Percy angrily. It was unlike the other dragons, it had a long body and long feathers coming out of its upper nose, Percy had no clue what it was, but he knew one thing he had found his last trial. He tried hitting it but the red dragon vanished in the blink of an eye, Percy could not pin it down. The angry beast appeared behind him and whipped him with its tail, Percy was sent flying but to his shock, he did not hit the wall and went straight through it. He fell on a grass field under the moonlit sky. Percy could not help but look at the giant pyramid-looking structures in the distance. As he was admiring the beauty of this place, a man patted his shoulder and said, "Welcome to Paradise." Percy turned around and said, "I'm not dead yet, am I?" Percy saw a lanky tall man with a healthy beard. He was wearing red robes but his most significant feature was his moustache. It was long, Percy had never seen such a long mustache on such a man. He replied, "Paradise is not a place, it's the people who make the place a paradise." Right after he finished, the man raised his arms, and grass walls rose in front of the duo. Percy said, "What is this?" The man chuckled and said, "That's for you to find out, the sky's the limit, Amigo" He snapped his finger and vanished straight away. Percy looked at the grass walls and contemplated his decision to agree to come with Vulcan because he had to explore things out of his comfort zone. He was never the kind of guy to think rationally, he wanted to kill and burn everything. This quest made him realize that actions have consequences and nothing can be undone. It made him realize the importance of patience and calmness, two things that he had never thought about before but now he was in a stalemate. Percy touched the grass wall and a gateway opened up, followed by a path. He started walking down the said path and ended up on the right turn. He kept on walking but could not find the end of this maze. Percy soon realized that he would get nowhere by aimlessly running around. He was exhausted and had to sit down. He began to think about all the possibilities that could happen, he became even more tired and laid down on the grass and stared at the starless sky. It was strange that it was such a beautiful place but the stars were not decorating the sky, as he was thinking about it he saw a star glowing brightly. Percy quickly got up and stared at it. It was not quite above his head. He knew that it was the only thing in this web of grass. Percy started following the star and tried to get underneath it, after many turns and dead ends he finally got there and saw something, a green glow in the distance. He rushed to it like a hungry lion to his prey. It was a green gem, an emerald? No, it was much prettier.

Percy stopped and admired it for a moment, he could not take his eyes off it. He slowly walked towards it and his face lit up by the glow of the beautiful jewel. As soon as he touched it, he teleported back to the room where he was before. He looked to his left and saw the red dragon charging in, he had to jump over it. He looked closely and saw the head of the dragon was glowing, it had a green glow in the middle of its head. He landed and took the gem out of his pocket, it was glowing. Percy knew what he had to do. He unsheathed Hofund and struck it in the ground, he stepped back and let the dragon come to him. As soon as the flying beast started flying towards him, Percy charged towards his sword but rather than grabbing it, he used it as a boost to launch him above the dragon, he saw an opening and put the gem on its head. It made a loud explosion which could be heard outside the room. Vulcan was alarmed and slowly walked towards the door. Hardly had he reached it the dragon flew out of it knocking Vulcan down. Vulcan saw Percy riding it as it flew past him. He was happy for Percy. He landed near the sorcerer and said, “This is amazing but this dragon is different not like the ones I have heard about.” As he said the dragon suddenly vanished. Percy was surprised and looked at Vulcan searching for an answer. He said, “It's not any dragon it’s the Quetzalcoatl, the Mexican dragon. It was hidden here by me. It possesses immense power that no one could harness at the time, not even me.

It requires someone with the same hunger and strength that the dragon has. You need to become one with the Quetzalcoatl. You can summon it at any time you want, just call its name and it will appear from the green gem you found. Percy said, "You know about the gem as well." Vulcan nodded and said, "I designed that maze myself. You will be amazed at the things I know. Now let's go to Alessandra." Vulcan raised his arm and a chunk of the land they were standing on rose, as they came up they saw Percy and heard the screech of an eagle. He looked upwards and saw Ikaros circling the volcano, his eyes swayed down on Alessandra and saw her standing with Angelos. Percy did not know what to say, Angelos dashed to him as a speedster would and said, "Sparta is under attack. Aetios asked me to inform you. We can get there in a day if you allow me take you on my back." Percy chuckled, he pulled out the green gem, looked at it, and said, "I've got a different plan."

Chapter 15

FOR SPARTA!

Theseus took Solaris, Nathan, and Atreus to the map room and said, “We have men on all sides of the city but one of us needs to be on each front. Solaris said, “I agree, if Deimos is to attack with full force, swords, and shields will only get us so far we will need something special.” Nathan said, “B… But what can I do, alone?” Theseus said, “There is always something one can do, we just need to look inside of us. I insist that you command the front near the sea that way you might be able to use the water to your advantage.” Nathan replied, “But I have never used water as a weapon.” Solaris said, “Then you will have to now. There is no time for ifs, but or maybe’s, we need to act now.” Atreus remained quiet but still had doubts in his mind about the war. Theseus said, “Solaris on the east, Atreus on the west, and I will be on the northern battlefront. Let’s prepare Spartans, war is upon us whether you want to accept it or not." All of them left the room to prepare for the inevitable clash with Deimos. It was a strange time for Nathan and Atreus as they had never fought in an all-out war whereas Solaris roamed the Greek lands all his life and had no time for anything else. Theseus's body was filled with adrenaline at the thought of a war, as the chief of the spartan army he had witnessed many wars, he had nothing to lose but his pride. Solaris went straight to a cliff near the castle after leaving the map room. He sat down on the cliff and started talking, "The day I lost you, I thought that I had no purpose in life but after all this time I finally feel like I have a direction in life. I need to help them with the powers I have been granted. I hope you are proud of me." He had tears in his eyes, as he got up and turned around, he saw Atreus standing in front of him. He was stunned. Atreus said, "Who were you talking to?" Solaris wiped the tears off his face and said, "I was just talking to myself, nothing else." Atreus replied, "You need to tell me, how can we be a team if we can't rely on each other?" Solaris nodded and said, "Everyone has got something in their lives that didn't go as it was supposed to. For me, it was Greta, the girl I could give my life for. She was the shadow of my light, one day she died because of me. I could not save her. Deimos sent his dogs to attack me but I was not there, so he killed her. Ever since I have been trying to make things right." Atreus was speechless, he could not comprehend the pain Solaris had gone through. Solaris said, "Leave it for now, if she was here she would also want us to do the same." Atreus and Solaris walked into the castle once again and saw Nathan doing random hand movements in front of a glass full of water. Atreus said, "Have you gone insane?" Nathan shamefully put his hands behind his back and said, "Nothing I was just trying to control water. I thought that if I practiced it now I would not feel awkward afterwards." Atreus started laughing, as he was laughing a soldier came rushing in and said, "Sir, they are coming in from the west." Solaris and Nathan looked at Atreus as he suddenly stopped laughing, his face changed from a happy kid to a concerned adult. Solaris said, "Go now, and remember it's not the power that you possess but the heart you own." Atreus immediately left the room, Nathan looked at Solaris and said, "Think we should go too." Solaris nodded his head and replied, "I agree, that would be a wise decision."

Atreus quickly arrived at the walls of the west front and saw the archers raining arrows from above, he quickly ran up the stairs and saw Adonis who was one of his friend trying to stop hundreds of creatures running towards the gateway. He joined the archers and started shooting arrows, but nothing was fazing them. It was like if one is killed two more come running down, they had reached the walls and started climbing up them. Atreus shouted, "I need men on either side to get them off the wall." The

Spartans tried their hardest to stop them from climbing the walls. Atreus could not fathom the situation, everything was happening simultaneously. He looked down and saw a pile of creatures just lying on the foot of the wall. He thought to himself about all the stories he had heard about wars and warriors of Sparta, it was much more painful than he expected it to be. As he was thinking about that he heard a voice shouting, "They are trying to breach the gate." Atreus thought, "But how can these creatures breach a big gate." He looked down and saw about ten men with a battling ram, smashing it to create an entry, to his surprise he could not see too many creatures near them. Atreus looked back, grabbed a rope, and said to Adonis, "Cover me, I will take them out." He tied the rope around one of his arrows, looked Adonis right in the eyes, and jumped off the wall. Adonis could not believe what he saw, Atreus fired an arrow which got stuck in between the wall. He looked down and saw Atreus running on the wall with the help of a rope and then jumping down behind the people ramming the gateway. Atreus landed on the ground and saw the people carefully, they had black smoke in their eyes, it was completely abnormal. They started running towards him, and Atreus started shooting arrows continuously, one of them grabbed him by the foot and said, "No one will survive, I am coming to get him." Atreus quickly recognized the voice and said,

"Deimos? How can he be… we will need reinforcements quickly."

Solaris had also secured his battlefront by a wall of light which when crossed burnt everyone's skin. Nathan's battlefront had no movement, it was like they didn't even know about this entrance.

Theseus on the other hand was standing in front of the gateway alone. He had ordered everyone else to leave this front to him. He stood there with his eyes closed and waited. Amid the silence, he heard a voice say, "I should have expected, it would be you." Theseus opened his eyes and said, "I could not give this joy to anyone else." He saw Deimos with a black hooded robe come out of the trees, "Sparta will crumble today and it will start with you." Theseus pulled out his sword and said, "Then so be it."

Chapter 16

THE HIER OF POSEIDON

Although Nathan had not seen anyone yet, he was still spectical of the fog that surrounded the sea. He recalled seeing a similar type of fog when he was in Taenarum. Nathan quickly alerted Omiros who was a fellow spartan standing right beside him, "Omiros, I think they will attack from the river." Hardly had he said that when he saw rocks on fire flying out of the fog. Nathan shouted, "Brace for impact." They were hit very hard by the first attack, he knew he had to do something. Nathan put his hands forward and tried to form a wall of water in between them but he could not hold it properly. The rocks went through the wall and started hitting the spartan soldiers. Nathan was horrified. "No, this is all because of me. I need to do something about it." As he was about to bring his hand down a rock came flying towards him. He froze on the spot and closed his eyes immediately, he could didn't do anything but nothing happened. He slowly opened his eyes and saw Aetios standing in front of him with the spear in his hand, "Zinovia, you might want to take this one, I will be there in a moment." Zinova helped everyone get to cover. Aetios grabbed Nathan by his arm and took him behind a pillar near them. Nathan was mumbling, "It's my fault. It's my fault." Aetios interrupted him and said, "No, it doesn't matter if it's your fault or anyone else's fault. Are you ready to fight? Are you? I just need to know because the city is under attack and we don't even know what we are fighting against and I've got a Spear. None of this makes sense but I am willing to fight because it's my duty to protect Sparta but I can't do my duty if I am worried about you. It doesn't matter what you were or what you did, the only thing that matters is that are you willing to fight if not I suggest you stay here but if you step foot on the battlefield, you are a Spartan." Nathan was stunned by his words, Aetios left him there and went back out to help Zinovia. He pulled out his spear and threw it towards the boats in the river, quickly teleporting to them he started striking them down but he saw something odd, their eyes were blacked out. He quickly remembered the man he saw in Delphi, "They are innocent people, Deimos is controlling them." He shouted, "Zinovia do not shoot them." Zinovia was confused but believed in his decision. Aetios knew he could not kill them but it was quite hard when they were constantly attacking him. He tapped the wolf head on his spear and the blade changed into a blunt head. Aetios said, "Zinovia, shoot their legs, just incapacitate them." He started throwing light blows to the controlled people, they started falling unconscious one after another. He cleared the boats one at a time but it wasn't enough. The boats breached the wall a little bit but it was enough for Deimos' army to get through. Aetios teleported back to top of the wall to Zinovia and said, "We need to stop them from getting inside the city." Aetios threw the spear down among the creatures and as he teleported a golden glow surrounded him, he said in a low voice, "Wolf Mode." Aetios transformed once again but this time the stakes were higher than ever. He started slashing through the bloodthirsty monsters. They outnumbered him massively, Aetios could barely keep up with the pace of the war. The creatures started piling up on him, he could barely see Zinovia shooting arrows from above the wall. It was looking unlikely that they would be able to stop the attack.

Nathan was sitting behind the pillar watching it all unfold. He wanted to help but did not know how, he closed his eyes, sat down, and said, "Poseidon, help me. I don't know what to do." Hardly had he said that, he heard a deep voice say, "I was expecting to see you for a long time." Nathan opened his eyes and saw a tall man with a strong beard standing in a dense forest with a stream running nearby. He was wearing blue robes with a golden pendant shaped like a trident. He continued, “I see you have not been training.” Nathan had his head hung down in sorrow and said, “What can I do, I am not as powerful as Aetios and Percy. I cannot do what they can do in a war.” Poseidon sighed and said, “Is that what you think? If yes, then you are completely wrong. Water covers the majority of the world, more than any other element. You cannot even fathom the power you contain inside of you.” Nathan nodded in disagreement and said, “But, I am just a tracker.” Poseidon waved his arm upwards, summoned some water in a mug, and poured it in the stream, “Water has no identity, it can take up the shape of anything, it evolves over time to suit its surroundings. If you do not understand this quick enough, many lives will be lost.” Poseidon put his finger on Nathan’s head and showed him a vision. He saw Thermopylae covered in blood, and soldiers lying dead everywhere, among those faces he saw Aetios, Percy, and Eivor. He was shocked to see his friends in such a state, “What can I do to save them now.” “You need to become one with the water, but for now you are not ready. Allow me to show you the power of the Sea God.” Poseidon put his hand on Nathan’s shoulder and vanished instantly.

Aetios was about to pass out when he heard a voice say, “Get off him.” Zinovia saw pieces of water fly towards the creatures but she could not see anyone. Aetios got up, smiled, and said, "I knew it." Nathan walked out of the smoke, his eyes were blue and he had a water bubble surrounding him. The creatures tried to attack him but could not get close to him. Nathan raised his hands and started flying in the bubble of water, Aetios and Zinovia could do nothing but admire as he called upon the water from the sea. It took the shape of a giant blue bull, made out of water and ready to ram through everything that came its way. It could be seen all over the city, Solaris looked at it and instantly knew who it was, "The Cretan Bull, what a sight." It started charging through Deimos' army, and Aetios and Zinovia quickly got out of the way. Nathan demolished every single creature on the battlefield, the bull was stamping on everything in its path. The boats on the other side of the wall started retreating, the aqua animal stopped and vanished slowly, Nathan descended into his bubble. Aetios ran to him and found him unconscious. Zinovia said, "Leave him to me. Go and help the others." Aetios was about to leave when he saw a mace come flying towards him, he barely dodged it, "We meet again" said Dunamis as he walked out from the broken wall. Aetios looked closely and saw Pyrrhus and Kari walking on either side of the mace wielder. Aetios banged his spear on the ground and said, "I will finish it properly this time." Pyrrhus and Kari flew in from left and right respectively and Dunamis charged straight down the middle in order to capture Aetios. The eagle visioned was in quite a predicament when he saw something, an opening. If he struck at the right time he could get all three of them at once. Aetios leaped into the air immediately, the evil siblings clashed with each other while trying to capture him. While in the air, Aetios threw the spear at Dunamis, which he dodged immediately. Aetios chuckled and said, "You don't learn, do you?" He teleported behind Dunamis and cut his mace off the chain, this made him angry. He shouted and Aetios saw him get bigger every second and fog started collecting all over the battlefield. Aetios looked behind him and saw Pyrrhus and Kari holding a sword to Zinovia's throat, "We will kill her if you don't surrender now." Dunamis's voice changed into that of a monster, "You are not leaving this place alive." Aetios could not think of anything when he saw a bright light flying down towards them. Kari said shockingly, "What is that?" The light crashed onto the ground making a huge explosion that knocked everyone back. As the rays shimmered away Aetios saw Vulcan standing there. He raised his arms and started rotating them clockwise, water and rocks started collecting in a circle. Pyrrhus and Kari got pulled into the mix, Vulcan quickly diverged his arms in opposite directions and the duo were sent flying out of the city. He said, "Did I miss anything?" Aetios had a huge smile on his face and said, "Where is Percy?" Alessandra walked in and said, "He has gone to help Theseus. I will take care of Nathan, The rest of you should go to the northern battlefront." Vulcan looked at the transformed Dunamis and said, "Yes, you can go, I will deal with our friend over here."

Chapter 17

THE DRAGON AND THE WOLF

Eivor went straight towards Theseus but little did he know that Deimos was already there. Both of them started exchanging blows, the evil one was a bit surprised by Theseus's resistance, "You have still got it, old man." He put both his hands up and called upon a lightning strike from the clouds, Theseus pulled out his sword, deflected it onto the tree beside him, and said, "I have learned much since our last encounter." Deimos conjured his scythe and replied, "I am killing that boy today, one way or another." Theseus swung his sword in the air, "In that case, I will fall first." Theseus ran towards Deimos but he slammed his scythe on the ground and made clones of himself. Theseus stopped at once and looked around him, he could not find anything that suggested the real one. Every clone started attacking him one after the other, Theseus could do nothing but dodge their attacks but one of them hit him and left a deep wound. All of the clones chuckled and said, "Give up now or you will experience the wrath of darkness." Theseus heard the screech of Ikaros in the sky, "Give up? I have still got a few things up my sleeve." He whistled loudly and the golden bird came flying down and sat on his forearm. A bright light engulfed them, Deimos could do nothing but look as his clones disappeared. As soon as he opened his eyes, he saw Theseus had transformed, he had golden wings on his back. He started gliding all over the place to confuse Deimos, but he was adamant about killing him. The evil one started sending bolts of lightning toward the flying messiah but could not even touch him at that speed. Theseus came flying in towards Deimos, grabbed him by his head, and flew up, "Don't even think for a second that I would let you touch my city." He dive-bombed with Deimos smashing into the ground head first.

Vulcan stood in front of a mutated Dunamis, "Let's see what you've got." The giant charged up his hand to attack on head-on. Vulcan lifted from the ground with air and started circling him. Dunamis grew angrier, he started swinging all over the place. He did not have a clue where Vulcan was, the elemental master but to fingers to his lips and blew fire out of his mouth which hit Dunamis right in the eyes. Vulcan landed back on the ground and said, "Let's finish this now." He waved his arms in the air and summoned water out of thin air, he directed the water to cover Dunamis. Vulcan then blew cold air and froze the giant in its place. Zinovia was amazed upon seeing him make such easy work of one of Deimos' generals. Alessandra said, "We need to take Nathan by the river, he needs water."

Eivor turned up at the exact moment, he was shocked to see such a big explosion. Theseus walked out of the smoke, he looked injured, "Late, again? Tell me you've got them." Eivor quickly reached into his belt and pulled out the Blades of Hades, "I don't think we will need them." Theseus spat blood on the floor and said, "Deimos is darkness itself, he cannot be killed. We have to seal him." As soon as he said this both of them heard Deimos, "That was something. I can tell why all the nations fear you." He got up, banged his scythe on the ground and a swarm of Skyloi came running in from the forest. Skyloi was the dog-like creature that had attacked them many times before. Theseus said, "We need Aetios here, where is he? I will keep Deimos occupied. You will have to take care of the Skyloi." The Evil One saw the Blades from a distance and said, "Oh! so you have got the gift of Hades, well in that case I will have to end it quickly." Theseus flew off the ground and landed in between Eivor and Deimos, looked him right in the eyes, and smiled. Eivor started slicing through the Skyloi one after the other but they were overpowering him in number. The Soul keeper remembered Hades's words, he put both ends of the blades together and made a clone of himself. They both fought collectively and the Skyloi had little chance of winning. Theseus on the other hand was very exhausted and could only stall Deimos from entering the city. The Evil One charged towards Theseus with his scythe, the spartan could do nothing but block his attacks. Eventually, Deimos struck down the sword from his hand, Theseus was completely vulnerable. Eivor had dealt with the Skyloi, he looked over to the duo and saw Deimos had his scythe held high up and was about to cut off Theseus's wing, "NO, Stop." He threw his blade at Deimos but it was not enough. He had cut his wing off when the blade hit him, Eivor ran to Theseus and held the spartan in his arms, "No, no, no. Breathe, Theseus." Deimos got up again and said, "It's your turn now, boy." Deimos walked closer to Eivor. He once again put his scythe up and was ready to strike him down when The Spear of Leonidas landed between both of them. Deimos was flabbergasted, "What?" A golden glow surrounded the spear and Aetios said, "I will never let my comrades die." A ball of fire came flying in from the right and hit Deimos right in the face. Eivor said, "Aetios… Percy…" Percy saw Theseus lying in Eivor's arms and said, "Take him to Alessandra." Deimos got up and said, "It's very kind of you to walk into your death." Percy replied, "And it's very stupid of you to think that you could take over Sparta." Aetios struck his spear on the ground and transformed. The golden armor appeared once again, "Let's do this." The duo charged towards Deimos and one after the other started exchanging blows. The Evil One was blocking everything. He pushed them back with his scythe and struck them with consecutive lightning blasts. Aetios was sent flying by one of them but Percy blocked them all. Deimos said, "You still do not have the weapon of the God of War. You cannot stop me." Percy smiled and said, "For now, this will do." He reached for the emerald, tapped it once and the Quetzalcoatl appeared behind him, making him look like a God. Aetios got up and was not amazed to see the dragon as he always believed Percy to do well under Vulcan's guidance. Percy said, "Come on, let's do this our way. The Wolf and the Dragon has a nice ring to it." Aetios smiled and joined forces with Percy. The fire-heart mounted the dragon and flew in from above while Aetios charged in from the ground. Deimos was startled to see the Quetzalcoatl. He remembered his visit to Delphi, he had seen it, and his end was destined to be a dragon. Aetios threw his spear at him which hit his shoulder. Percy jumped from above with his sword aimed at Deimos' head but as he was about to hit him, Deimos vanished away into a black hole leaving the Spear on the ground. Percy said, "No! where has he gone?" Aetios calmed Percy and said, "He will return, we need to check on Theseus." Both of them ran towards the others, Aetios saw everyone gathered around Theseus' body. Solaris was there with Atreus, Vulcan, Nathan, Alessandra, Zinovia, and Eivor. Percy knelt and said, "Theseus, forgive me I couldn't save you. If I had been a fraction quicker, it might have ended differently. You were the best mentor I could have asked for." Everybody was in tears when Atreus said, "Look, something is happening." A bright light came out of Theseus's chest and Ikaros flew out of it, everyone's faces changed from sorrow to hope but that hope quickly changed into delight when Ikaros said, "I am not dead, yet." Confusion was a similar feeling among the crowd. Solaris said, "Don't tell me…" Theseus replied, "Yes, I had split my soul into two pieces and Ikaros was my other half, while my body is dead the other half of my soul is still alive." Aetios came forward and said, "Thank Zeus, you are still with us but we need to move quicker now, Deimos will not sit quietly after what happened today." Theseus agreed with his student and said, "Yes, I think we will need to split up into three teams, that way we can cover more ground. I found a scroll containing information on the other weapons but I have only deciphered their names as it is a thousand years old. Vulcan and Alessandra will accompany Percy to find The Sword Of Ares. Solaris will partner with Atreus in the search for The Bow Of Artemis. Zinovia, Aetios and me will help Nathan find The Trident Of Poseidon. Deimos will do everything in his power to create the strongest army to take us down but I say we take the fight to him. What say you?" Aetios, Percy, Eivor, Nathan, and Atreus shouted, "HO!!" "Get ready then, as now time is our greatest enemy."